CHRISTMAS BABIES FOR THE ITALIAN

CHRISTMAS BABIES FOR THE ITALIAN

LYNNE GRAHAM

MILLS & BOON

First published in Great Britain 2020
by Mills & Boon, an imprint of HarperCollins*Publishers*
1 London Bridge Street, London, SE1 9GF

www.harpercollins.co.uk

HarperCollins*Publishers*
1st Floor, Watermarque Building, Ringsend Road
Dublin 4, Ireland

Large Print edition 2021

© 2020 Lynne Graham

ISBN: 978-0-263-28831-5

MIX
Paper from
responsible sources
FSC
www.fsc.org FSC C007454

This book is produced from independently certified FSC™ paper to ensure responsible forest management. For more information visit www.harpercollins.co.uk/green.

Printed and bound in Great Britain
by CPI Group (UK) Ltd, Croydon, CR0 4YY

CHAPTER ONE

SEVASTIANO WAS ON the very brink of a satisfying sex-fest with a lissom blonde model when his mobile phone interrupted him. Usually he would've ignored it, but that particular ringtone had been programmed in by his sister and it was distinctive. And Annabel would never call him late at night unless something was wrong.

'Excuse me… I have to take this,' Sevastiano intoned, stepping back.

'You're joking.' The tumbled beauty assumed a baffled resentment, her ego clearly dented by his retreat. On the other hand, getting a technology billionaire into her bed was a coup of no mean order and had to have *some* drawbacks. She forced an understanding smile, because women adored Sevastiano and there was a lot of competition out there.

Certainly Sevastiano Cantarelli hadn't been standing unseen behind any door when his looks had been handed out at birth. Six feet four inches tall, he was broad of shoulder and lean and powerful in build, and the exquisite Italian designer suits he wore were perfectly tailored to his lithe, muscular frame. Olive-skinned and black-haired, he was blessed by dark deep-set eyes that gleamed like liquid bronze in the low light.

'Annabel?' Sevastiano probed anxiously.

Frustratingly, he couldn't get a word of sense out of his kid sister because she was distraught, sobbing and stumbling over her explanations. He did catch the gist of the story: some huge family drama that had apparently seen her told to leave the paren-tally owned apartment she inhabited and deprived of her car. Could she move in with him?

Sevastiano rolled his magnificent eyes at the idea that she would even have to ask such a question. She was the only member of his English family whom he had ever cared about. He still remembered the shy and loving little girl who would slide her hand comfortingly into his when their mother was referring to him regretfully as her 'little mistake' or her father was shouting at him.

'I'm sorry I have to leave…a family emergency,' Sevastiano told the blonde without a shade of hesitation.

'It happens…' Donning a silky robe, the model slid off the bed to see him out.

'Dinner tomorrow night?' Sevastiano suggested before she could speak.

She was beautiful, but many women were beautiful and yet still none could hold Sevastiano's mercurial interest for longer than a month and few for even that long. Courtesy, however, was as integral to his nature as his attachment to his half-sister.

In his limo being driven home, he wondered what on earth could have happened to eject Annabel from her family's good graces, because his sister never argued with anyone. Sevastiano had left the Aiken family and social circle of his own volition and he knew he hadn't been missed. From birth to adulthood, after all, he had been the embarrassing reminder that his mother had given birth to another man's child. He had *never* belonged. He had always been an intruder, the dark changeling when everyone else around him was blonde, and a high achiever when mediocrity would have been preferred. Those harsh truths no longer bothered Sevastiano. After all, he didn't like his snobbish, shrewish mother or his power-hungry, bullying stepfather, Sir Charles Aiken. He had even less in common with his half-brother, Devon, the pompous, extravagant heir to his stepfather's baronetcy, but he genuinely cared about Annabel.

So what on earth could she possibly have done to enrage her family? After all, Annabel avoided conflict like the plague. She followed the rules and stayed friendly with everyone, no matter how trying their behaviour. Only when she had insisted on training in art restoration had she defied the Aiken expectations. Her mother had wanted a daughter who was a socialite and had instead been blessed with a quiet, studious young woman devoted to her museum career. What could've happened to distress his half-sister to such an extent? Sevastiano frowned, conceding that he had spent a great deal of time in Asia in recent months and consequently had seen much less than he usually saw of Annabel. Obviously he was out of the loop...

And once Annabel had flung herself, sobbing, into his arms at his elegant Georgian town house, confessions, recriminations and heartfelt regrets tumbling in an unstoppable flood of revelation from her tongue, Sevastiano realised that he had been so far out of the loop that he might as well have been on another planet and that the situation was much more serious than he could ever have guessed.

Annabel had fallen madly in love with a much older man and had an affair. Sevastiano was even more shocked to discover that she had met the man concerned at one of his parties: Oliver Lawson, not a friend, a business acquaintance.

Sevastiano compressed his lips with a frown. 'But *he's*—'

'Married… I know,' Annabel cut in, dropping her head because she was too ashamed to meet his eyes. She was a tall slender blonde with large reddened blue eyes and a drawn complexion. 'I know that *now* when it's too late. When we met he told me that he and his wife were legally separated and getting a divorce… I believed him. Why wouldn't I have? His wife lives at their country house and never ever comes to London and there was no sign whatsoever of a woman at his apartment. Oh, Sev… I swallowed every stupid lie and excuse he gave me.'

'Oliver may be CEO of Telford Industries, but his *wife* owns the business. I would say it is very unlikely that he would divorce her. Lawson must be twice your age as well!' Sevastiano said in frank consternation. 'His life experience made it even easier for him to take gross advantage of your trust.'

'Age is just a number,' Annabel mumbled heavily. 'I feel so dirty now. I would never have got involved with him if I'd known he was still actually living with his wife. I'm not that kind of woman—I believe in fidelity and loyalty. I really loved him, Sev, but I can see now that I was a complete fool to believe his every word and promise. When I told him that I was pregnant, he tried to bully me into going for an abortion. He kept on phoning me and demanding that I do it and then he turned up at the flat to underline that he didn't *want* this child and we had a huge row.'

'You're pregnant,' Sevastiano murmured flatly, striving to hide his rage from her because the concept of any man trying to browbeat Annabel into an abortion outraged him, particularly a man who had already lied and cheated his way into an inappropriate relationship with her. At twenty-three, his sister was still rather naïve, very much prone to thinking the best of everyone and making excuses for those who let her down. Obviously, she should never have got involved with Lawson in the first place while he was still married, but then his sister didn't have much experience with men outside a first-love relationship at university with a boy-next-door type.

Even so, had she ever taken a clear unbiased look at the men in her own family circle perhaps she would have been less trusting. His mother and her father weren't faithful to each other although they were very discreet. Her brother was married and a parent but had still enjoyed a lengthy affair with another married woman. Indeed, growing up, Sevastiano had witnessed so much infidelity that he had not the slightest intention of *ever* getting married. What would be the point? While he retained his freedom as a single man, he had nobody else's needs to consider and he liked his life empty of family obligations and commitments and all the complications that went with them. Annabel and his birth father were the sole exceptions to that rule. That aside, however, he would still never have treated a woman as Oliver Lawson had treated his sister.

No intelligent man with an active sex life ignored the daunting possibility of an unplanned pregnancy and Sev had never run that risk with even a moment of carelessness, a track record he was proud to recall. But if anything *did* go wrong, it was a man's responsibility to behave like an adult and support the woman's choice, regardless of his personal feelings, he reflected grimly.

'So, I womaned up and went home and told Mama and Papa about my baby and they went crazy!' Annabel gasped, covering her convulsed face with her hands again. 'I expected them to be upset but *they* want me to have a termination as well and when I refused they told me I had to move out of the apartment and hand my car back. And that's fine…it really is. If I'm not living the way they want me to, I can't expect them to help me out financially.'

'They're trying to bully you as well,' Sevastiano breathed tautly. 'Nobody has the right to *tell* you to have a termination. I gather that you want this baby?'

'Very much,' Annabel confirmed with a sudden dreamy smile. 'I don't want Oliver any more, not since finding out that he's a liar and a cheat, but I still very much want my baby.'

'Having a child alone will turn your life upside down,' Sevastiano warned her. 'But you can depend on me. I'll sort out another apartment for you.'

'I don't want to depend on anyone. I have to stand on my own feet now.'

'You can work on that goal once you've got yourself straightened out,' Sevastiano told her soothingly. 'You're exhausted. You should go to bed now.'

Annabel flung herself into his arms and hugged him tight. 'I knew I could rely on you to think outside the box. You don't care about gossip and reputations and all that stuff! Mama says I'm ruined and that no decent man will want me now.'

'That sounds a little strange coming from a woman who married your father while carrying another man's child,' Sevastiano murmured grimly.

'Oh, don't let my stupid mess take you back down *that* road,' Annabel urged unhappily. 'This is a completely different situation...'

And so it was, Sevastiano acknowledged after his sister had gone to bed. His Italian mother, Francesca, had been on the very brink of marrying Sevastiano's Greek father, Hallas Sarantos, when she had met Sir Charles Aiken on a pre-wedding shopping trip to London. In Annabel's version of the story, Francesca and Sir Charles had fallen hopelessly in love, even though Sevastiano's mother had only recently realised that she had conceived by Hallas. In Sevastiano's version of the story, Francesca had fallen hopelessly in love with Sir Charles's title and social standing and his stepfather had fallen equally deeply in love with Francesca's wealth. Two very ambitious, ruthless and shallow personalities had come together to create a social power alliance. Sevastiano would have long since forgiven both his mother and his stepfather for their choices, had they not denied him the right to get to know his birth father, who had strained bone and sinew to gain access to him, only to be denied for the sake of appearances.

What had happened to Annabel, however, *was* unforgivable in Sevastiano's estimation. A much older married man had taken advantage of his half-sister and had then tried to intimidate her into having a termination against her will, a termination that would have neatly disposed of the evidence of their affair. And Oliver Lawson would *pay* for his sins, Sevastiano promised himself angrily as he contacted a top-flight private investigator to request a no-holds-barred examination of the other man's life, because everyone had secrets, secrets they wanted to keep from the light of day. Sevastiano would dig deep to find Oliver's secrets and work out where he was most vulnerable. He was pretty certain that Lawson had not the smallest suspicion that Annabel was Sevastiano's half-sister, because he was a connection that the Aiken family never acknowledged.

The man, however, had seriously miscalculated when he chose to deceive and hurt the younger woman. At some stage of his existence, such a self-indulgent man would have made a mistake with someone else and Sevastiano would uncover that mistake and use it against his target in revenge. Sevastiano cared for very few people but he cared very deeply for his only sister, who had been the one bright spot of loving consolation in his miserable childhood. As long as he was alive neither she nor her child would ever want for anything but, first and foremost, Oliver Lawson had to be *punished…*

Humming under her breath, Amy rearranged the small shelf of Christmas gifts in the tiny shop area of the animal rescue charity/ veterinary surgery where she worked. The display made her smile because she loved the festive season, from the crunch of autumn leaves and the chill in the air that warned of winter's approach to the glorious sparkle and cheer of the department-store windows she sometimes browsed in central London.

She had a child's love of Christmas because she had never got to enjoy the event while she was growing up. There had been no cards, no gifts, no fancy foods or even festive television allowed in her home because her mother had hated the season and had refused to celebrate it in even the smallest way. It had been at Christmas that the love of Lorraine Taylor's life had walked out on her, abandoning her to the life of a single parent, and she had never got over that disillusionment. She had always refused to tell her daughter who her father was, and the devastating row that Amy had caused when she was thirteen by demanding to know her father's identity and refusing to back down had traumatised both mother and daughter.

'He didn't want you! He didn't want to know!' Lorraine had finally screamed at her. 'In fact, he wanted me to get rid of you and when I refused he left me. It's all *your* fault. If you hadn't been born, he'd never have left me…or even if you'd been a boy, a *son*, he might have been more interested. As it was, in *his* eyes, we were just a burden he didn't need!'

After that confrontation, Amy's already strained relationship with her mother had grown steadily worse. She had started hanging out with the wrong crowd at school. She had stopped studying and had got into trouble, failing her exams and ultimately wrecking her educational prospects. She had hung out with the kids who despised swots, had begun staying out late, playing truant, skipping her assignments and lying about her whereabouts. It had been childish stuff, nothing cruel or criminal, but her mother had been so enraged when the school had demanded she come in to discuss her wayward daughter's behaviour that she had washed her hands of her child. Amy had ended up in foster care until a kindly neighbour and friend had offered her a home if she was willing to follow rules again.

It had taken several years for Amy to recover from that unhappy period when she had gone off the rails and she had never lived with her mother again. Lorraine Taylor had died suddenly when her daughter was eighteen and only afterwards had Amy discovered that the father who had abandoned them both had been supporting them all along. Although they had never lived anywhere expensive and her mother had never worked, Lorraine had still contrived to go on cruises every year and, while she had resented spending anything at all on her daughter, she had always had sufficient funds to provide herself with an extensive wardrobe. In fact, Amy had been stunned by the amount of money her mother had had to live on throughout the years of her childhood but none of that cash had been spent on her. That financial support had ended with Lorraine's death and the solicitor concerned had reiterated that Amy's birth father wanted no contact with his child and wished to remain anonymous.

Aimee, she had been named at birth… *Beloved*, Amy recalled with rueful amusement, but, in truth, she had not been wanted by either parent. Perhaps her mother had thought the name was romantic; perhaps when she had named her daughter she had still harboured the hope that her child's father might return to her.

Even so, it wasn't in Amy's nature to dwell on those negatives. Cordy, the kindly neighbour who had taken her in and soothed her hurts, had taught her that she had to move on from her misfortunes and mistakes and work hard if she wanted a decent future. At a young age, Amy had wandered into the animal shelter next door to the block of flats where she and her mother lived and had stayed on to see the inmates, soon becoming a regular visitor. Cordelia Anderson had been the veterinary surgeon who ran the surgery/rescue charity, a straight-talking, single older woman, who had devoted her life to taking care of injured animals and those who were surplus to requirements. She had nursed the animals back to health, rehoming them where she could.

She had taken in Amy when she was at her lowest ebb, persuading the unhappy girl to pick up her studies again, and had even tried to mend the broken relationship between Amy and her mother but, sadly, Lorraine Taylor had been quite content not to have the burden of a teenager in her life. When Amy had finally attained the exams she had once failed, Cordy had taken her on as a veterinary nurse apprentice at the surgery. Tragically, Cordy had died the year before and Amy had been devastated by the suddenness of her demise. Amy was still doing vocational training as an apprentice for Cordy's veterinary surgeon partner, Harold, and praying that she could complete her course before Harold retired.

Since Cordy's death Amy's home had become a converted storeroom above the surgery because Cordy's house had had to be sold, the proceeds going to her nephew. Amy used the shower facility in the surgery downstairs and cooked on a mini oven in her room, while acting as caretaker for the shelter at night. But making ends meet had become an increasing problem for her because she was on a low salary and was now responsible for covering her own living expenses. To supplement her income, she had taken a job as a waitress in a café nearby and worked shifts there when she wasn't required at the surgery.

The café, decorated in the style of an American diner, enjoyed a clientele from the office buildings that surrounded it and was often busy, but the following day when Amy turned up for her shift it was almost deserted because the rain was bouncing off the pavements outside.

'If this weather keeps up, either you or Gemma can go home,' the owner, Denise, told her with brisk practicality. 'I don't need two waitresses here with no customers.'

Amy tried not to wince and just nodded,

knowing that Gemma, a single parent, was as in need of her pay as she was. Days off didn't settle the bills or the cost of travelling on the bus and home again without earnings to cover the expense. But that was the fatal flaw in casual labour, she acknowledged ruefully—it didn't promise either regular shifts or a steady income. A job dependent on the vagaries of the weather or the number of customers was, at the very least, unreliable. Still, she reminded herself doggedly, it wouldn't be the first or last time that she spent a week eating instant noodles because paying her electric bill or buying new scrubs to work in was more important.

'Gemma's not due in until the lunch shift so maybe business will have picked up by then,' Denise told her consolingly.

As she spoke the door flew open and a man appeared, a very tall and broad-shouldered dark-haired guy with raindrops spattering the pale raincoat he wore over a business suit. He took a seat in the corner and Amy got her first good look at him and fell still.

She didn't usually stare at men but he was so drop-dead, utterly beautiful that she allowed herself a second glance, expecting to pick up a flaw, a too large nose, a heavy jawline, something, *anything* to make him less than perfect because nobody, absolutely nobody aside of airbrushed magazine models and movie stars, could possibly be that perfect in real life.

But *he was*, from his high sculpted cheekbones to his classic nose and wide, sensually full mouth. A trace of dark stubble shadowed his carved jaw, emphasising his perfect mouth and eyes as dark and golden as melted molasses. Luxuriant blue-black hair, worn a little longer than was conservative, framed his lean, darkly handsome features and then Amy unfroze as she felt the visual assault of those brilliant dark eyes locking to her and he signalled her with a graceful brown hand.

Of course he was signalling her. He was in a café and she was a flipping waitress! The scarlet heat of intense embarrassment invaded what felt like her entire body, burning her up inside and out with the most overpowering awareness she had felt since she was an ungainly teenager. Almost clumsily she moved forward, horribly conscious of her stupid frilly uniform for the first time ever, and asked how she could help him.

'A black coffee, please,' he murmured, the faint fluid edge of a liquid foreign accent curling round the syllables in his dark deep voice.

'Anything else?' Amy settled the menu down in front of him with a hand that trembled slightly.

'I'm not hungry enough for a meal.'

'Something sweet?' Amy proffered shakily, indicating the cake cabinet behind her.

'I think you might be all the sweet I could handle right now. But, *sì*, something sweet... You choose for me,' he urged sibilantly.

Amy wheeled away, her face still burning, wondering what he had meant about her being sweet. She probably *looked* like a sweet in the pink frilly collared dress and apron she had to wear to work at the café. Denise made the coffee and watched her choose a cake from the cabinet.

'A case of insta-love or whatever you young ones call it these days?' her employer teased.

'What do you mean?'

'Well, you stopped dead to look at *him* and he hasn't taken his eyes off *you* once since he came in. Go ahead and flirt. It'll give me something to watch.'

'I don't flirt with customers,' Amy said tightly.

'I'm almost fifty and I'd flirt with *him*, given half the encouragement he's giving you,' Denise said drily.

Sevastiano watched Oliver Lawson's daughter with keen attention. She didn't match his expectations of a former rebellious adolescent who had ended up in foster care: he had expected more attitude, a harder visible edge than she seemed to possess. She looked almost alarmingly innocent but that, he told himself, was probably a front. He had his plan, a simple plan, and to make it work he *needed* Amy Taylor to play a starring role.

Yet what he hadn't counted on was the bolt of pure masculine lust that had gripped him the instant he laid eyes on his quarry and saw the name tag, 'Amy', on her uniform. She was tiny and curvy with silky golden hair swept up in a long ponytail, little tendrils framing her heart-shaped face, and the most extraordinary eyes, a real living doll. He didn't think he had ever seen that shade of eyes before, a remarkable violet-blue that glowed against her porcelain skin. There had been no photo of Amy Taylor in the file and he had not expected her to be a beauty, but she was. It would make it easier for him, he told himself, because he wouldn't be faking desire for her.

For the merest split second, Sev's conscience twanged. He was going to take an ordinary girl out of her element and give her a whirl and in no other circumstances would he have considered such a move. While the world might consider him a player, he only played with women who knew the score. But he would show Amy a good time and give her a break from her dreary workaday world, he told himself impatiently, exasperated by that instant of doubt. She would enjoy herself. A young woman of twenty-two didn't look for much more than fun from a man. It was not as though he intended to have sex with her— no, he would not be taking the illusion *that* far, because he wasn't quite that cruel—but he *would* be using her as a weapon against the father she had never met.

'May I treat you to a cup of coffee?' Sev asked as she approached him with his coffee.

'Go ahead,' Denise encouraged Amy, putting her on the spot when she would have politely turned the request down.

After all, Amy didn't really 'do' men in any sense. Even when she was a teenager, dating had been a nerve-racking disappointment. She didn't like being grabbed or mauled by men who were virtual strangers, and had soon realised that the overly large bust and generous behind she possessed, combined with her small frame, generally attracted the wrong sort of male attention and attitude. She wasn't the type to jump into bed on a first date either but that seemed to be the expectation from most men she met. After a couple of distressing experiences with men who didn't like taking no for an answer, her rosy dream of finding a man of her own, a best friend and lover combined, had died. As a rule, she avoided noticing flirtatious signals and kept her life simple, as she saw it, because she was perfectly happy without a man. Indeed, she literally didn't have a space in her busy work schedule for one.

His dark scrutiny felt intense as she slid behind the table to sit opposite and she ducked her head, murmuring awkwardly, 'This is not something I do… I mean, sit down with customers.'

Dio mio, she was shy, Sev registered in wonderment, inclined to view her as though she belonged on an endangered species list. 'Tell me about yourself,' he urged with greater warmth, seeking to instil confidence and trust.

Colliding with gorgeous liquid-bronze eyes enhanced by inky black lashes, Amy felt butterflies break loose in her tummy and her mouth ran bone dry. Denise slid her favourite coffee onto the table and quietly retreated back behind the counter like a woman unexpectedly finding herself watching a live soap opera. 'I like animals more than people,' she heard herself confide, and inwardly winced at that opening sally tripping off her paralysed tongue.

'As do I. What sort of animals? I like horses.'

'I'm fondest of dogs although I like cats as well. I'm training to be a veterinary nurse. It's an apprenticeship and between the surgery and the rehoming charity that runs from the same base and working here, I don't have much time for other interests. What's your name?' she heard herself ask breathlessly.

And it wasn't even a little surprising, she acknowledged, that she was finding it a challenge to catch her breath that close to such a spectacular guy.

'Sev, short for Sevastiano. It's Italian,' he told her, frantically wondering how on earth to make her relax in his company because nothing he usually said or did with other women seemed to work on her. Accustomed to women who came on to him simply if he smiled, Sev was in foreign territory because when he had tried to compliment her earlier by calling her sweet, she had visibly closed down and backed away, more intimidated by his interest than anything else.

'I thought I heard a bit of accent…er…not that it's that noticeable or anything,' Amy hastened to add, afraid she shouldn't have commented in that line, fearful it was rude.

'So, you work for an animal rescue charity. That's interesting. I'm looking for a dog,' Sev informed her lazily, setting that last fear to rest. 'I would like to have a pet.'

Amy's heart-shaped face lit up and shone as though he had announced he could walk on water. The violet eyes sparkled and for the first time she lifted her head and awarded her whole attention to him. 'What a coincidence!' she exclaimed without any shade of irony.

In fact, looking directly into those wide open expressive violet eyes, Sev didn't think she would be capable of sarcasm. On some level that gentle sincerity reminded him of Annabel, but he shoved that thought out of his head as soon as it appeared. She seemed to be a nice, if possibly naïve, young woman, so naturally he was a little out of his comfort zone, but he wasn't planning to harm her in any way…was he? Through him, she would discover the identity of her father and possibly even pick up a little more gloss—nothing damaging about those developments, he assured himself smoothly.

'A very convenient one though,' Sev commented. 'Presumably you know all the dogs currently in the shelter?'

'Well, first and foremost, there's Hopper, who's getting old and only has three legs,' Amy told him, reddening from inner discomfiture because she adored Hopper and didn't want anyone else to take him home, which was selfish, as she often told herself.

'Oh, yes… I could—' she began with animation, until the sound of the door opening and the voices of new customers sent her head twisting round and she rose in haste to do her job. 'Sorry, I have to work,' she told him apologetically.

Sev sat over his coffee for several minutes, oddly content, he discovered in surprise, to watch her darting about serving people. She was fast on her feet and quick to smile, exceedingly cute even to his cynical appraisal and noticeably evasive when other men tried to chat to her. And every so often her bright gaze would dart back in *his* direction, as if to reassure herself that he was still around, before swiftly retreating again. *Sì*, she was hooked, Sev recognised with all the skill of a wolf. She was way too young for him, of course. And when the truth came out, as it certainly would at her father's country house party, she would be shocked…or maybe not, he reasoned carelessly. Maybe she didn't much care who her absent father was; she could hardly have much invested in the idea of a man she had never met.

To be fair to her, he would compensate her in some way afterwards, he decided abruptly. He would not simply *use* her, he would *reward* her for her unintentional assistance. Satisfied by that decision, every concern laid to rest because, when it came to the female sex, Sev believed that sufficient money or a very generous gift could assuage any ill or offence caused, he pushed his coffee cup away and slowly rose to his full height, approaching the counter to settle his bill.

Amy landed at the counter to hand over an order almost simultaneously and, although he was not at all vain, Sev didn't think it was a coincidence. 'Sorry, we were interrupted. Where is the shelter you work at? Perhaps you could organise a visit for me,' he suggested.

The violet eyes lit up and glowed and Sev, who rarely smiled, smiled and absolutely dazzled her. She hovered, momentarily in a daze, and blinked up at him, muttering the name and street the shelter was on, information that he naturally already knew but had had to request to maintain his pretence.

'This evening, perhaps,' Sev added, seeing no reason to waste time with the party only a couple of weeks away.

'Er…y-yes,' Amy stammered in a near whisper. 'I'll be back at the shelter between four and six. I could show you the dogs and see if there is one who suits.'

'See you then,' Sev completed, turning on his heel to head for the exit.

'I *told* you he was interested,' Denise hissed over the counter after passing the food order back to the kitchen.

'Yeah,' Amy muttered ruefully. 'In acquiring a dog, not a girlfriend. A guy like that wouldn't go for someone like me.'

'I think you're wrong,' Denise carolled.

But Amy didn't argue because she knew she was right. She didn't have what it would take to attract a man of that calibre, neither the looks nor the stylish sophistication. Indeed, she thought it was absolutely typical that she had finally met a man who did attract her, only to discover that he was more interested in acquiring a pet. A man who was interested would simply have asked for her phone number, wouldn't he?

CHAPTER TWO

AMY WENT HOME after her shift finished, the rain having stopped and business having picked up sufficiently for both her and her fellow waitress to have stayed on at work.

Harold, the vet for whom she worked, was just finishing up in theatre with the nurse, Leanne. Amy suppressed a sigh, knowing that she would have to do the post-operative clean-up required and she was already tired. Leanne was a pleasant woman but she never did any physical work when there was someone more junior on staff, particularly someone like Amy, who did not have the luxury of working set hours. Amy had been hoping to get the chance to tidy herself up a little before Sev arrived but, if he came early, that prospect was now unlikely.

An hour later, already wondering if he

would visit at all or if he was simply another one of those random people who said they wanted a pet but never actually got around to getting one, she hurtled into the shower room, already reckoning that Sev would fail to appear. Why had she got so excited anyway? Even if he did come, he would only be looking at the dogs, not at *her*, she reminded herself in exasperation.

But what was it about him that had grabbed her interest so strongly that she had felt weirdly intoxicated when he'd actually spoken to her? So thrilled she could barely vocalise? So excited that she was embarrassed for herself? Obviously his sheer magnetic attraction had played an initial part in her reaction. But there had been something more, something she had *never* felt before with a man, a deeper hunger to get to know who he was, how he functioned, how he thought… oh, just everything about him. Dumb, she told herself impatiently, because even if he did visit, it wasn't her that he was interested in, was it? So, she was being childish and silly weaving dreams about the poor man, who for all she knew went home to a wife and a bunch of children after work, quite unaware that he had wowed the waitress out of her apparent single brain cell!

He hadn't been wearing a wedding ring though, because she had somehow checked that out the instant she'd sat down at that table, but not all men chose to wear a ring, she reflected, thoroughly irritated with her thoughts and her one-track mind as she raced upstairs to her room to get dressed and apply a little make-up. Why? Well, miracles *did* happen, she conceded with a rueful smile, because Cordy had been Amy's very first miracle, entering her life again when it was a mess and bringing her into her cosy home and *loving* her. Nobody had ever loved Amy before and Cordy's love and support had been transformational for her in every way.

Attired in jeans and a blue sweater, she went downstairs to the shelter to feed the animals. Volunteers came in several days a week and cleaned the kennels and walked the dogs. Some animals at the shelter were old tenants, those deemed unlikely to be re-homed for various reasons. She let Hopper out of his cage, and he danced around her in rapturous welcome, his lack of a fourth leg not inhibiting him in any way, but he quietened down quite quickly because he was no longer a young animal.

For all intents and purposes, and only behind closed doors, Hopper had become Amy's pet, who slept in her bed every night and loved her as much as she loved him. But practically speaking, Amy couldn't take Hopper on officially because few landlords allowed pets and as soon as she completed her apprenticeship in four months' time, she would have to find other accommodation. Her right to live above the surgery had been Harold's solution to her completing her training on low wages but the surgery *would* need the room restored to its former use.

Six o'clock had come and gone, and Amy had long since abandoned hope of Sev appearing when the downstairs bell rang. She blinked in surprise, wondering who it was, hoping it wasn't an abandoned animal or anything that would prevent her going to the evening class she had to attend at seven. It wouldn't be the first time someone had rung the bell and left a dog tied to a lamp post outside, and then she would have to phone Harold and stay behind to attend to the practicalities of a new arrival with him. She clattered back downstairs, wondering when on earth she was likely to get the time to eat.

The vision of Sev waiting outside knocked her for six because she had assumed he was a no-show, and suddenly being presented with him again when she had least expected it was unnerving. She took a harried brief glance at him, noting that he had changed into jeans and a dark green sweater, teamed with a jacket. 'Er…you can come in but we'll have to be quick because I have to go out,' she warned awkwardly.

'I'm sorry… I'm late. I had to stay on at the office to take a phone call,' Sev told her truthfully, assuming that the explanation of her having to go out was merely an excuse of the face-saving variety and untrue.

'Luckily, I'm still here for a little while,' Amy told him cheerfully, leading him out through the back of the building to the kennels. 'Well, meet the residents. Those three at the top end are not available for various reasons and the same goes for the lower four cages.'

'What reasons?'

'Kipper bites when he gets nervous, which is most of the time. Harley only responds to commands given in German—he's very well trained but it puts people off—and Bozo, the bald one, is still receiving treatment for a skin complaint,' she explained, standing back to watch Sev stroll down the path between the cages, viewing all the animals, a motley crew of bulldogs, terriers and cross-breeds.

Simultaneously, she was also taking in his broad shoulders and narrow waist while noting how his incredibly well-fitted jeans showcased lean hips, muscular thighs and long, long straight legs.

He had the strong, healthy physique of an athlete, she thought helplessly, conscious of the tight pulling sensation tugging at her core, which she had never felt before, and flushing pink as her nipples tightened almost painfully inside her bra. Surprise darted through her as Hopper trotted up to him and pushed against his knee. Sev stretched down an absent hand and massaged Hopper's flyaway ear.

'And this little chap?'

'Oh, that's Hopper, he's *really* old,' Amy muttered, knowing that Harold would be furious if he heard her say that to any patron seeking a pet because Hopper was as in need of a good home as any of the other inmates. 'Well, he's only ten, and the three legs don't hold him back or give him any problems,' she added in a guilty rush, inwardly praying that Hopper would not be chosen and loathing herself for that piece of selfishness.

She hovered at the entrance and was completely unprepared to hear Sev start talking to Harley in German. At least, it sounded like

German to her because Harold knew a few basic words of the language and it sounded the same. She watched as Harley perked his ears up in pleasure and sat down, stood up, lay down, performed a circling excited motion and then completed his audition by sitting down again.

'Harley and I seem to be a match. Can you let him out of the cage for a minute?'

In haste, Amy checked her watch. 'It will only be for a minute. I have to leave soon,' she reminded him.

'To go where?' Sev fenced.

'I have a class to attend. It's part of my apprenticeship. I usually attend day release every week, but this is a revision class for a final exam.'

'That's unfortunate because I was about to ask you to join me for dinner this evening,' Sev advanced smoothly.

Disconcerted by that unexpected invitation, Amy tensed but Cordy's careful lessons on self-discipline and focus kicked in. 'I'm sorry. I would have liked that, but I can't risk failing anything in my course. I have to complete it by the spring because my boss plans to retire then.'

The liquid-bronze eyes that were so stunningly set in his lean, hard-boned face narrowed in intensity as if he was surprised by her refusal. In the uneasy silence that fell, Amy crossed to Harley's cage and unlocked the door. 'Just a few minutes,' she warned. 'I'm afraid if you want Harley, you'll have to come back to fill out the forms for him.'

Inside herself, some small part of herself was bouncing up and down with excitement that he had actually *asked* her out. Her pale skin went pink and Harley's boisterous greeting to his prospective new owner was a welcome icebreaker. With a couple of words, Harley was settled down again by Sev.

'He *is* very well trained,' Sev acknowledged of the Labrador, still reeling in shock from the first rejection he had ever received from a woman. So that she could attend a *class*, of all things? That astonished him. He looked at her, savouring the fall of long golden silky hair tumbling round her tiny shoulders in disarray, the brightness of her eyes, the full luscious pout of her pink lips. As she arched her back in her effort to quietly persuade Harley back into his cage, his keen gaze locked to the generous swell of her breasts and the tight denim stretching across a bottom the shape of a ripe peach. He went hard as a rock and inwardly swore, turning away for a moment to look out of a window without a view because it was dark. He didn't know what it was about her, but she made his body react with all the involuntary enthusiasm of a teenage boy and that set his teeth on edge.

'So, you *are* interested in Harley?' Amy summed up, walking back towards the exit in the hope of giving him a polite reminder that time was short. 'My boss, Mr Bunting, will be here every day but Sunday. He's the only person able to sign a dog out of the shelter.'

'Understood,' Sev murmured, glancing back at Harley and deciding that, yes, he would go through with the adoption. In the short term, Amy might want to come and visit the dog and that would suit his purpose. In addition, he had an entire household of staff, who were under-utilised with only him to look after: they would walk the dog, feed it and look after it.

'I should warn you though…' Amy said hesitantly. 'Harley's a bit of a cuddle monster.'

'A…*what*?' Sev pressed with a frown.

'He's used to attention and being a companion dog. His owner was young and died suddenly, maybe spoiled him a little,' Amy proffered, wondering if she should've kept quiet as his lean, darkly handsome profile grew thoughtful.

'No, that won't bother me,' Sev assured her immediately because he never allowed anything or anyone to bother him. He supposed that *he* was a little spoiled since he had become rich enough to pay employees to take all the annoyances out of his daily life. 'But right at this moment, I'm more interested in you than Harley.'

'*Me?*' Amy gasped, her throat tightening.

'And which evening we're going to get together for dinner this week,' Sev extended lazily, reaching down...and down—*Dio, she was short!*—to tuck a golden strand of hair behind her ear as she stared up at him with those wondering violet eyes. Absolutely mesmerising eyes, he registered uneasily, stepping back for a split second before he could think about what he was doing, which was an unnerving experience for a guy who calculated his every move with cool, steadfast precision.

Those long brown fingers merely brushing lightly against her cheekbone during that tiny manoeuvre felt shockingly intimate on Amy's terms. Nowadays she almost never had the comfort of any kind of physical contact with anyone. She shivered in reaction, staring up into his lean sculpted face to clash with glittering liquid-bronze eyes. Giddiness assailed her and her breath grew short in her throat while her body suddenly became uncomfortably warm.

'Er…this week,' she began shakily. 'That could be a little difficult. I'm on duty at the surgery most evenings until nine, so I won't be free until Friday.'

And even being that available would mean skipping a shift at the café, she reminded herself guiltily, and she really couldn't afford to take that financial hit. Still, she would only be young and foolish once, she told herself soothingly, couldn't always strive to be careful and sensible, particularly not when a man as extraordinary as Sev strolled centre stage into her life.

'Friday will do fine,' Sev assured her calmly, inwardly amused by her intensity, the open book of her little face that clearly proclaimed her attraction, her longing, her elation. He would make sure she had a good time, he assured himself smoothly, buy her something, *spoil* her. She would have no regrets when he walked away again. 'I'll pick you up at eight. We'll do dinner and a club.'

Barely able to think straight as the door closed on his exit, Amy raced back upstairs to collect her coat, and it could not be said that her revision class that evening received quite the attention it was due because she was already frantically wondering what the heck she would *wear* on Friday. She didn't own a socialising wardrobe, only casual stuff, couldn't even recall when she had last put a dress on. But she certainly couldn't afford to buy anything, unless it was out of a charity shop and even buying there was sometimes beyond her budget.

In the end it was her fellow waitress and closest friend, Gemma, who came to her rescue on the clothes front with several outfits that the older woman urged her to borrow. 'I used to be out every weekend,' she had said with regret. 'But once you have a child, it changes things.'

Recalling that conversation, Amy sighed, for once grateful that she had had her mother's caustic example to guide her through the challenging world of relationships. Although she had never learned the details, she had always assumed that her mother had fallen accidentally pregnant and had, at an early age, resolved never to put herself in a similar position with a man. For that reason, even though she was still a virgin, she had recently gone on the pill, reasoning that sooner or later there would surely be a significant someone in her life and that it was better to be safe than sorry.

The outfits Gemma loaned Amy were mostly too tight or too long because the two women were not similar in size, but Amy finally selected a stretchy black velour dress with a lower neckline than she would have preferred but which was cut short enough to suit her height. She pressed tissue into the toes of the black glittery stilettos she had borrowed and stuck her feet in them at the last minute, fussing with her freshly washed hair and tweaking her light make-up until she heard the doorbell. Her heart was banging at about fifty times a minute before she even answered the door.

It disconcerted her to find a strange man in a smart suit on the doorstep and her attention flew past him to the limo waiting at the kerb. 'Mr Cantarelli is waiting in the car, Miss Taylor.'

Amy simply froze, staring beyond him in disbelief at the uniformed chauffeur holding open the passenger door of a very long glossy car and regarding her expectantly. She gulped and made her shivering way across the icy pavement into the warm, inviting depths of the very first limousine she had ever travelled in.

Sev dealt her a cool look of appraisal and a faint smile that failed to light up his eyes this time and she noticed the difference, immediately wondering if he was already regretting asking her out now that he had seen her dressed up to the very best of her ability.

'The limo,' she said jerkily. 'You should've warned me. I didn't realise it was you... Who was the man who came to the door?'

'A member of my security team.' Sev scanned her, taking in the sheer glory of the petite curvy figure beside him. A body to die for, he acknowledged hungrily, absorbing the pale smooth swell of her cleavage, the slender knees and ankles, her gorgeous face and even more appealing smile. Even though she looked on edge and nervous, she was impossibly cute. And he didn't *do* cute, didn't know where he had even found that word in his vocabulary, and it didn't matter that she had the breasts of a goddess, *he* wouldn't be going anywhere near them, he reminded himself impatiently.

'What's wrong?' Amy asked worriedly, catching the frown that briefly pleated his black brows. 'Is it the dress? Isn't it smart enough? I borrowed it.'

Shut up, shut up, close your mouth and don't gabble, she was telling herself as that embarrassing admission of insecurity tumbled from her lips.

'Who from?' Sev enquired, initially intrigued by the idea of her in borrowed finery even if it made him appreciate that he would have to buy her a presentable dress for the Lawsons' big pre-Christmas party. Of course, she wouldn't have the money for something like that. No, he intended to choose the optimum moment to unveil her identity. At the same time, it annoyed him that Oliver Lawson's daughter lived in such poverty compared to her father. Surely Lawson could have helped her out beyond the level of paying child support? Amy Taylor had had to struggle even to complete her education after a less than promising upbringing.

'Gemma, she's a friend,' Amy framed, striving to look back levelly at him and calm down, and utterly failing in that aspiration because she was so overpowered by both him and her deluxe surroundings that she felt as though she were trying to function in some strange dreamscape.

'Would you like a drink?'

'Yes, please…that would be great,' she declared, trying not to gape as a liquor cabinet operated by a button emerged from the plush leather and glass division between driver and passenger. But when he uncorked a bottle of pink champagne there was no hiding her consternation.

'Are you celebrating something?'

'Hopefully the moment when you relax,' Sev told her lazily.

'Well, you could be waiting a long time for that,' Amy admitted ruefully. 'Right now, I feel as though I've walked onto a movie set. I'm not used to this level of extravagant living.'

'I'm still the same man,' Sev murmured.

'But what on earth are you doing with me?' Amy countered. 'I don't fit in your world.'

'Never try to define me by my income. We live in the *same* world.'

'Doesn't feel like it, right now,' she admitted tautly as he passed her a moisture-beaded glass brimming with bubbling palest pink liquid.

She sipped, grateful to have something to occupy her restless hands, and by the time they arrived at the world-renowned hotel where they were to dine she was on her second glass, taking even tinier sips to carefully control her alcohol intake while encouraging

Sev to talk. And my goodness, getting Sev to talk at all, she discovered, was an uphill task.

Asked about his day, he muttered, 'Work… meetings,' and that was that. Asked to tell her about something that had annoyed him, he looked at her with a frown and claimed that it took a great deal to annoy him. Asked to describe one positive development, he looked downright blank, and he said drily as he walked her into the hotel where he was greeted by name by the uniformed doorman, 'Where are you trying to go with these strange questions?'

'My foster mum, Cordy, used to tell me to think of something positive to say about every day, especially if it was a *bad* day,' she stressed wryly, struggling not to react to that revealing word, 'strange'.

Sev gritted his teeth because he thought that was a terrible idea. 'Be careful or I will christen you Little Miss Sunshine. There was nothing positive about my day. It was stressful.'

But as she gave him a forgiving smile for

that honesty, he knew he had lied. She was probably the most positive development in his day because she made negativity and pessimism a challenge, he acknowledged ruefully. They were polar opposites in character. Sev knew himself to be dark right down to his innermost soul and a case-hardened cynic. He expected the worst from people. He let nobody get close to him. He might be attached to Annabel and his birth father, Hallas, and his happy family, but he confided in none of them. What he thought and felt, he kept strictly to himself because it was safer not to let anyone get too close and learn too much about him. His childhood had taught him the art of self-protection. Even Annabel, in her innocence, had betrayed him once or twice with her loose chattering tongue.

He could still recall sitting at the Aiken dinner table when he was ten, the evening his half-sister had chosen to announce that *he* was unhappy at boarding school. Even better did he recall her sobbing incomprehension as the parental storm of rage had broken over his head while he was shouted at and humiliated for his ingratitude as though he were some charity case taken in off the street. He could never have dreamt then that, in point of fact, his birth father was a wealthy man, who would have given him a home in a heartbeat or that, as his heiress mother's firstborn, he would come into a substantial trust fund of his own at twenty-one. No, his mother and stepfather had instead combined to make him feel frightened, defenceless and unwanted in the only home he had ever known.

Amy's gaze was wide as she scanned the opulent hotel foyer and the member of staff, the manager, no less, who came forward to personally escort them into a magnificent dining room. Conversations faltered, heads turned to look as they were shown to a central table and she was horribly conscious of her inexpensive dress and lack of jewellery, already wishing that Sev had chosen to take her to eat somewhere less public and more private. At the same time, she was scolding herself for such thoughts because it was a huge treat to be taken out somewhere fancy for a meal and the superb surroundings should only add to the thrill of the experience.

That aside, however, one glance at Sev's taut dark features and the hardness in his dark shadowed eyes warned her that Sev's thoughts had taken him somewhere he would rather not have gone, and she was wondering if she had said something unfortunate until he asked her about the shelter and how she had first become involved with it. She told him about visiting the animals when she was a kid, getting to know Cordy, and in passing she mentioned her difficult relationship with her mother, for the shelter had often acted as an escape hatch when she had displeased her only parent.

'Why didn't you get on with her?' Sev probed, surprising her, because for a man who didn't want to talk about himself he seemed very keen for her to do the opposite.

'It wasn't just me who struggled to get on with her,' Amy divulged reluctantly. 'She had a sharp tongue and she often offended people. My father dumped her when she was pregnant, and she never got over it. She was really bitter. Remember Miss Havisham in *Great Expectations*? Mum didn't sit around in the wedding gown she never got to wear but she still kept it in her wardrobe...'

Sev rolled his eyes. 'That must've been difficult.'

'I got through it and then Cordy offered me a home,' Amy told him, glossing over her time in foster care, when she had lived in a council-run home for teenagers deemed troublesome.

'It seems that you owe your foster mum a great deal,' Sev conceded.

Amy could not resist telling him about the good work Cordy had done with the charity, animation lighting up her face as she discussed the animals she loved. She talked a lot, Sev conceded, but what she talked about held his interest, unlike the women who chattered to him about fashion designers, social events and their own fascinating selves. A waiter topped up her wine glass with a discreet hand.

Most crucially, Amy was not obsessed by herself *or* her appearance, Sev acknowledged. She walked past mirrors without looking at them, paid no heed to the men noticing her and fussed with neither her hair nor her make-up. Yet the more Sev studied her, scanning the perfect symmetry of her features and her flawless skin, the violet depths of her sparkling eyes and the pouty sexiness of her pink lips, the more he recognised her beauty. She might be very small, in fact downright tiny in terms of height, but she was undeniably gorgeous.

'You're staring,' she told him breathlessly.

Sev nodded, a sudden grin flashing across his wide, sensual mouth. 'I enjoy looking at you, *cara mia.*'

Her cheeks flamed at his directness even as a warm feeling mushroomed in her chest and she dropped her head and fiddled with her wine glass. She wished she had the nerve to tell him that she liked looking at him too, indeed could barely take her eyes off the sculpted angles and hollows of his lean, darkly handsome face. The meal was beautifully presented and wonderfully tasty and when she stood up to leave she felt pleasantly full and mellow in mood. A knot of excitement tightened low in her belly when she met his liquid-bronze eyes and marvelled at the lush inky lashes that enhanced them.

A crowd of people were milling outside the upmarket club. She had heard of it because the name appeared frequently in the gossip columns, it being the sort of exclusive venue generally only attended by the rich and famous. The women she glimpsed on the way in seemed very polished and the clothes they wore were elegant, slinky and revealing. In her plain black dress, she felt mousy and funereal, and as a queue stand was removed for them to move upstairs to the VIP area she tensed even more. A cocktail adorned with cherries already awaited her and she ate the cherries slowly, aware that she was already a little merry after the wine over dinner following on the champagne. Her attention was stolen by the semi-nude dancer on a little platform sinuously twisting and moving to the beat of the music. It was a very sexy display and she turned her head away to concentrate on Sev instead, surprised that his attention was still on her and not on the dancer.

'I wish I could dance like she can,' she said with a rueful grin.

Sev smiled, megawatt charisma blazing from that slashing smile because he had believed he had heard every possible comment on that performer from other women, every one of whom had viewed the dancer as competition and had found some excuse to denigrate her or her performance. But Amy, he was beginning to appreciate, did not like to speak ill of anyone. Why else did she call her late mother only sharp? According to the file he had, Lorraine Taylor had been, at best, a thoroughly dislikeable woman and an uncaring parent.

Sev rested an arm along the back of the

booth and angled his body towards her, his black shirt pulling taut across his muscular torso, his long powerful thighs slightly splayed, accentuating the bulge at his crotch. In spite of herself, her eyes were drawn there, and a curl of heat ignited in her pelvis because the force of attraction was so strong that, for the first time ever, she was seriously wondering...

In haste she lifted her head, her cheeks a heady pink, and she collided involuntarily with Sev's intent gaze and her heart skipped an entire beat before drumming back to life at greater speed, her tummy turning over as if she had gone down in a lift too fast. His hand eased down onto her shoulder and he urged her closer for his mouth to taste her parted lips. It was a shocking, seriously sexy manoeuvre because it was slow and measured, his lips firm and full and demanding while the rolling, twirling exploration of his tongue twinned with hers. She had never felt anything like the fierce hunger his mouth induced or the crazed surge of response racing up through her like a leaping flame, ripping through every defence yet bringing with it a sense of connection that she couldn't bear to deny.

The gradually deepening passionate intensity of that kiss sent her hands flying up into his hair, melding to his skull, fingering through the luxuriant strands of his dense blue-black hair to keep him close. Her body came alive with a great swoosh of feeling and she was astonished even more by how much she loved that adrenalin rush of sensation: the sudden urgent, almost painful tightening of her nipples driving the throbbing rise of liquid heat at her feminine core. She pressed her thighs together. It was all new to her and incredibly exciting.

Sev lifted Amy and set her back on the seat beside him because inexplicably she had ended up practically on his lap. Had he hauled her closer in the heat of the moment? Or had she approached him? He was breathing in quick shallow bursts, so aroused he was in pain and, while Amy had welcomed her response, Sev was fighting that overpowering need to the last ditch. He wondered if his overreaction could be laid at the door of his awareness that he could not possibly have sex with her. Did she have the magical allure of forbidden fruit? In the circumstances, touching her would be taking advantage because he was only faking his interest in her. And then, she *was* Oliver Lawson's daughter, he reminded himself squarely, so nothing intimate would be appropriate. Even so, those reminders did nothing to curb the aching pulse at his groin or his incredulity that any woman could push him so easily to the very edge of his control.

'Er...' Mortified to find herself almost reclining across Sev, wondering how the heck that had happened and if she had thrown herself at him in the midst of that kiss, Amy snaked back hurriedly into her corner, agonisingly conscious that her enthusiasm could have been misleading. She didn't like to give a man the wrong signals when she wasn't planning to follow through, and the conviction that he was probably now expecting her to go to bed with him that night forced her to tilt back her head and say stiffly, 'I'm sorry if I gave you the wrong impression but I'm not sleeping with you tonight.'

In receipt of that frank assurance, Sev stared back at her with wondering amusement firing his spectacular golden eyes. 'I don't know what sort of a man you think I am but I never put out on a first date.'

CHAPTER THREE

THE HELPLESS GIGGLE that forced its way up through Amy's tight throat erupted and she gasped for a breath of air before grabbing her drink and taking a hard swallow. Sev patted her gently on the back.

'Relax,' he murmured smoothly. 'No expectations here.'

Instead of being irritated by her warning, he had chosen to defuse her tension, had taken it in good part without embarrassing her. She smiled at him, her fears and insecurities laid to rest.

'So now you know all about me, why don't you tell me about you?' Amy dared, feeling surer of her ground.

His tangled background was a can of worms Sev had no intention of revealing, but he parted with the basic facts of his parentage in that his mother was Italian and his father Greek but that his parents had broken up before he was born and had married other people.

'That must've been challenging,' Amy commented, studying him with earnest violet eyes, and the luminous colour of them in the dim light only seemed to enhance her flawless creamy skin. 'I mean, having *two* fathers...'

'I didn't have two. My stepfather wasn't interested in taking on that role,' Sev divulged grudgingly. 'And I didn't meet my birth father until I had grown up.'

'Oh...' she breathed, glorious eyes rounding. 'I didn't have a father at all. He didn't want anything to do with me. Where did you go to school?'

'A northern boarding school when I was five.'

'Five's awfully young to leave home,' Amy chipped in, her surprise unhidden.

'I managed,' Sev told her, reflecting that was when he had first begun learning the power of self-sufficiency. As the only one of three children sent to boarding school, he had appreciated early on that he was the cuckoo in the family nest and he had stopped trying to change things, accepting the status quo until he was old enough to choose his own path.

'I can't imagine how,' Amy admitted with a faint shiver. 'I mean, my mum wasn't the milk-and-cookies sort but she was there for me when I was little.'

For a split second, Sev strove to picture his mother doing anything as maternal as offering comfort food to a child and he almost laughed at the concept, for Lady Aiken had never been a hands-on parent. At the same time, he was marvelling at how soft-hearted Amy could be and belatedly recognised that her chosen career looking after injured and homeless animals should have forewarned him, because that was in no way a glamorous role.

Keen to lighten the mood, he added, 'When I was older I was sent to an Italian school and

I enjoyed those years. My mother had cousins in the area, and I got to know some Italian relatives. I was able to go home to them at weekends and I was always made welcome.'

'It still sounds rather bleak and lonely to me,' Amy told him softly, studying him with troubled eyes.

And all of a sudden, Sev was wondering why he was even having such a conversation with her when he never talked about himself. Why on earth did she keep on asking such curious questions? He could not recall ever having similar chats on a first date. Women asked what age he had been when he made his first million or when he had lost his virginity and with whom, seeking information about his exploits and achievements rather than concentrating on the more personal stuff. Her curiosity about his childhood was oddly touching. He reached for her hand, strangely entranced by her small, slim fingers. 'I still don't have your phone number,' he told her, signalling the bar for fresh drinks. 'And you're not drinking your cocktail. Don't you like it?'

Amy dug out her phone and asked for his number and then sent him a text. 'I've had enough to drink for one evening,' she said ruefully. 'I don't have that strong a head for alcohol and I don't want to get drunk.'

She was so direct, and he wasn't accustomed to women who just said it as it was. He found it an endearing trait, but he definitely preferred more sophisticated women, who knew better than to ask awkward personal questions, he assured himself staunchly.

Fresh drinks arrived. She lifted the first one, which she hadn't finished, and sipped at it. She went to the cloakroom, reappeared with her pouty pink mouth freshly glossed and the instant he noticed he knew that he had to taste that strawberry flavour again. She sank down beside him and he tugged her closer with a relaxed grip and kissed her for the second time.

Instantaneously that fierce sense of excitement reclaimed her again and Amy quivered, struggling to keep her head clear, immediately blaming the alcohol she had imbibed for the way she was feeling. When he kissed her, the world stopped dead and flung her off giddily into an alternative universe where only the moment and the sensation mattered. Her fingers splayed across his shirt front, drawing in the heat of his virile chest beneath the fine fabric, the flexing of muscle as he bent over her and meshed long possessive fingers into the fall of her hair. Breathless and with her whole body humming like an engine, she was unnerved by the sneaking suspicion that she lost all control with Sev, a guy she barely knew, from a totally different walk of life. And because she never did anything without thinking in depth about it, she jerked back from him with an abruptness that sent his eyes flaring gold in surprise.

'I think we should dance,' she said tautly, needing to get a grip on herself, needing to know what she was doing, finally recognising that what was different was that, for the very first time, *she* wanted a man. But because she had never experienced anything that intense before the strength of her own response unnerved her.

'I don't really dance,' Sev muttered raggedly, lifting his drink and downing it in one gulp, grimly conscious of the erection tenting his neat-fitting trousers, a level of arousal he seemed not to be able to control around her.

'Then you can watch me,' Amy said cheerfully, entirely concentrated on gaining a necessary breathing space from him.

Taken aback, Sev watched her descend the stairs at full tilt without him. Amusement crossed the faces of his security team seated at a nearby table and the faintest colour scored Sev's exotic high cheekbones. As a rule, he didn't do PDAs. As a rule, he didn't kiss or indeed do much of anything with a woman in public. Why would he when they always took him home with them? No woman had yet said no; no woman had pulled away from him before. Even so, it definitely wasn't cool to be sitting in a club snogging Amy like a teenager, but then he had never found it so hard to keep his hands off a woman! He gritted his teeth and slowly stood up, the shock of her retreat and his bewildered incredulity having mercifully diminished his visible arousal. He strode down the stairs, located her at the edge of the floor and joined her with unmistakable reluctance.

Amy's breath caught in her throat as Sev appeared and her heart hammered at the sight of his tall, muscular body and wickedly beautiful features. She smiled at him because she had been afraid that he would be annoyed with her, had even feared that he might just walk out and leave her to find her own way home, because it wouldn't be the first time that her rejection of a man's advances had led to that unpleasant conclusion. In retrospect, she was embarrassed by her sudden departure from the table. For goodness' sake, he had only been kissing her! What was she that she had had to run away? Still fourteen years old and never been kissed before?

Well, never kissed like *that*, she conceded as they returned to the table and Sev acted as though nothing had happened and talked about working in Asia, where he had apparently spent most of the summer. He dropped her back at the shelter, climbed out of the limousine, towered over her and stared down at her.

'We'll do this again next week…if you like,' Sev tacked on belatedly, his self-assurance meteoric in comparison to hers.

'I like… I mean, I'd like that,' she muttered, hovering for a split second lest he wanted to kiss her again but not really surprised when he made no such move. After all, she had acted so jittery at the club when he'd touched her, he was probably reluctant to risk it again. What man liked being pushed away?

'Tell your boss I'll drop by tomorrow about the dog,' Sev added as she stuck the key in the lock.

'Yes. He's on duty all day tomorrow but, if you come early morning, you shouldn't have to wait long,' she advised him. 'Thanks for dinner.'

Unsettled, she went to bed and tossed and

turned while she mulled over the evening. In truth she was wondering if she would ever hear from him again or if she had already put him off. The prospect of never seeing Sev again already made her heart sink and she groaned, annoyed at herself for being too keen too quickly on a man who would never take someone like her seriously. She was on a hiding to nowhere, as Cordy used to say of hopeless cases. But even so, her brain still wanted to relive every little moment she had been with him, every second of those passionate kisses…and it was a long time before she got to sleep.

The next day, Sev had to cancel a meeting late afternoon to make his call on the surgery and express his interest in Harley. He did so, fully expecting to see Amy again. The more often he saw her, he told himself, the more likely it would be that she would agree to accompany him to the Lawsons' party, and he could only carry out his plan with her beside him…an unwitting *victim*? Well, he wasn't planning to do her any harm, he reminded himself afresh, had no idea why his motivation seemed to be faltering. No way could she be as soft and vulnerable as she appeared!

Furthermore, people liked to know certain facts about their background. Amy was only human and must always have wanted to know who her father was. Had she had the money she could have gone to court to demand to be told her father's identity, he reasoned impatiently. But she had neither the money nor the worldly knowledge to be aware that these days adults had the legal right to know certain facts about their parentage. *His* way, Amy would be getting that answer for free.

After a lengthy wait and filling out a welter of forms, Harley was bestowed on Sev. He sat quite happily on the end of the leash that Sev had brought with him while Sev endeavoured to casually enquire where Amy was.

'This is the day Amy attends her classes.' The older man studied him with a frowning look of assessment that Sev wasn't familiar with. 'She's a lovely girl. I've known her since she was a child. She's hard-working, honest and marvellous with animals but she's had a tough life,' he proclaimed.

'I gathered that,' Sev admitted, before taking Harley home.

Harley looked supremely unimpressed with the elaborate outside kennel that had been constructed that very morning for his occupation. The gardener, given a few necessary words in German, took him for a walk and then he was fed and shown into his fur-lined basket. Sev went out to see him, uncomfortably conscious of the mournful whining noise Harley emitted as he walked back into the house again. As Sev worked that evening in his home office, the vaguely audible whining slowly grew to a low-pitched howl that was very annoying.

'The dog won't settle,' his housekeeper informed him when he enquired. 'I think he's lonely.'

Guilt settled on Sev's broad shoulders and he let Harley out of the dog run. The Labrador pushed against him and looked up at him with adoring eyes. Sev worked while Harley snoozed peacefully on a rug but every time Sev stood up, Harley opened a suspicious eye to check on his new master's whereabouts. Lighting up the garden, Sev threw a ball for the dog, keen to tire him out before bed. Annabel came out to join him, enjoying Harley's antics because they had never been allowed to have pets when they were children.

Unfortunately, his sister's spirits had not improved much. He could see that she was working hard at putting on a brave face for his benefit but her haunted eyes told him that she was still devastated. She had loved and trusted Lawson and he had broken her heart. Tomorrow she would be moving into the apartment Sev had found for her near where she worked. He owned the entire building. He had suggested that she should consider staying with him a little longer, but she had insisted that she was looking forward to setting up her own home again.

'You're the best brother!' she told him with forced cheer as he put the dog back in the run. 'You're giving me a fresh start and that's what I need to shake me out of this fog of self-loathing.'

'Lawson took advantage of you, Bel. He lied. You have nothing to hate yourself for.'

'Except being stupid,' his sister interrupted, accompanying him back indoors as Harley loosed his first howl. 'Oh, dear, I hope he doesn't keep that up or none of us will get any sleep.'

'It's a matter of discipline,' Sev told her confidently.

'No, he doesn't like being away from you. He's a house dog, not an outdoor one,' his sibling told him ruefully. 'You really didn't think this through, did you? A pet is a *huge* responsibility.'

An hour later, Sev was gritting his teeth and still listening to Harley howl and when he couldn't stand it any more, he went downstairs and let Harley into the house. Harley accompanied him back upstairs to his bedroom and leapt on the bed. Sev exiled him to a far corner to lie down on the cushions he piled up for him. Harley lay down and sighed, propping his snout on his front paws and looking as pathetic as a dog could, but there was no more whining or howling and everybody got to sleep. Sev, however, wakened to find a large dog snoring on top of his feet.

Three days later, Amy studied her silent phone with annoyance. She was acting so juvenile about Sev and it exasperated her. She might never hear from him again, she *knew* that: she wasn't stupid. It happened all the time, according to her friends. A man could seem interested one minute and then forget your existence the next. That was just life and, with anyone, there was always the chance that another more attractive option offered and all the wishing and hoping in the world wouldn't change that fact, she reminded herself irritably. But would it be wrong or a dead giveaway to ask how Harley was turning out for him? Would that be pushy? Painfully obvious? Would it be chasing him? Amy agonised all morning over that issue and skipped her lunch because she felt nauseous and a little off-colour while still refusing to allow herself to think about Sev.

That evening, she felt really sick and wondered if it was the change of contraceptive pill she had been forced to request, but she soon realised that she must have eaten something that disagreed with her. She went to bed early with Hopper snuggled up to her and that was the most peace she got because she spent most of the night being ill, thumping up and down the stairs to the surgery washroom. She got up the next day, pale and with dark circles under her eyes but mercifully, no longer dizzy or feeling unwell. In a more brisk and practical mood triggered by Harold asking if she had heard how her 'friend' and Harley were getting on, she texted Sev and asked. It was only a polite enquiry, she reasoned irritably, wondering why she hadn't been able to find any trace of him on the Internet, reckoning that she was spelling his name, Kenterelli, wrong. But she could hardly ask him to write it down for her, could she? That would make her look stupid.

Sev smiled down at his phone and called her. 'Come and see Harley for yourself this evening,' he suggested. 'We can eat together.'

'I'm working until nine,' Amy admitted, suppressing a twinge of immature excitement and trying to keep her voice steady and calm.

'Not a problem. We'll eat later. I'll pick you up,' Sev asserted, tossing his phone on the desk. He would take her to an art gallery on Friday night and invite her to the party. On one level he was eager to get the party over with, on another he wished he had a few more weeks to play with.

Why? The less he saw of Amy Taylor, the better, he decided grimly, changing tack because he was realising that he was too susceptible to her sex appeal. If he was a bastard, he would just have sex with her to get her out of his system, but she deserved better. Regrettably his attempt to satisfy his libido with another woman the night before had failed. He had been in a weird mood though, he conceded with a bemused frown, inexplicably noting the unlucky woman's every flaw and, ultimately, unable to summon up sufficient interest to become any more intimate with her. That wasn't like him. Sex was generally just sex for him, not something his brain or his feelings got involved in. He wasn't and never had been the sentimental sort. In fact, it would have been more true to say that Sev viewed sex as an appetite to be assuaged on a regular basis, not a pursuit that required much thought beyond decency, safety and consideration. And then Amy had swum into view and sex had somehow become something that was ridiculously desirable but outrageously complicated and impossible.

And how had that happened? Lust was tormenting him for the first time ever because she was the very first woman he had wanted that he couldn't have. He was burning up for her as if she were his own personal Helen of Troy! She turned him on hard and fast. It was mindless but undeniable. It was also nonsensical, and he *knew* that and he firmly believed that it was *because* she was forbidden fruit. He knew that in the circumstances he could not sleep with her and that awareness made her all the more seductive a possibility. The sooner their association was over, the happier he would be, he told himself grimly, thoroughly exasperated by the introspection assailing him.

Amy rushed through cleaning the surgery, threw herself straight into the shower and ran upstairs in her bare feet to get dressed. Were they eating out? She hadn't thought to ask. Jeans and a top could well be too casual, but she didn't have much else in her wardrobe, having returned Gemma's dresses to her. In haste, she pulled on her most flattering jeans and a slightly shimmery blue top she had bought for the surgery Christmas night out the year before. She pushed her feet into canvas sneakers and dried her hair. The surgery bell went before she could even take advantage of her small stock of cosmetics and she groaned, scrubbing at her cheeks and her lips to give them a little colour, wishing she looked her best because Sev always looked amazing.

And Sev didn't let her down in that expectation. Sheathed in a black business suit, immaculately tailored to his tall muscular physique, he had teamed it with a dark red shirt that accentuated his olive skin tone and glossy black hair. A light covering of black stubble ringed his sensual mouth and jawline, enhancing his superb bone structure. He looked spectacular and her mouth ran dry as she climbed into the limo beside him and discovered that she would be sharing the space with Harley.

'You had him out with you?' she queried in surprise.

'Harley gets stressed when I'm not around. The vet says it's probably separation anxiety because his former owner disappeared so suddenly from his life, so I'm working on training him out of it with various strategies,' Sev assured her smoothly.

'Looks like he was lucky that he got you,'

Amy remarked, petting the quiet animal at her feet. 'He seems relaxed.'

'And my sister, Annabel, has offered to look after him when I travel,' he told her quietly.

'Everything covered. You're very organised,' Amy remarked, peering out of the windows as the traffic moved slowly past the bright sparkly windows of shops bedecked in their festive finery. 'I love Christmas. It makes me feel warm inside—'

'I'm not much of a fan. In my family home, it was never fun for children. Christmas was about formal entertainment for the adults.'

Amy nodded her head, guessing that by the sound of it he had been raised in a prosperous and educated household. 'Well, I never had a proper Christmas growing up because my mother didn't celebrate it, but that didn't put me off the whole season,' she confided. 'I know it's very commercial these days, but that doesn't stop me enjoying the traditional stuff like the carols and beautiful decorations or even the fact that most people smile more at this time of year. And the children are always *so* excited…'

'There are no children in my life.' Sev shook his head slowly. *'And* it's only now occurring to me that next year I'll have a niece or nephew to spoil. My sister is pregnant.'

'That's wonderful.'

'Sometimes, you can be a little naïve, *gioia mia*,' Sev countered. 'Annabel has no partner for support, she's on her own but for me… and the family, who mean so much to her, have turned their backs on her. This is a testing time for her.'

'But she's not alone as long as she has you and soon she'll have her child as well,' Amy responded calmly, undaunted by his critical comment. 'Everything has an upside and a downside. All that really matters is the way you choose to look at it.'

Sev widened his magnificent glittering bronze eyes in mockery. 'I'm of a more practical nature.'

'That's pretty obvious,' Amy riposted as the limo drew to a stately halt and Sev helped her out to stand in front of an enormous town house. '*This*…is where you live?' she prompted with dry-mouthed emphasis.

'I like a central location,' he said casually.

Amy swallowed hard and climbed the steps of the tall, classically elegant Georgian property, which she knew had to have cost millions of pounds. The yawning gap in their financial situations shook her rigid. Of course, she had guessed that he was well off when she first saw the limousine and the driver, but she had dimly assumed that that mode of travel could be a work-related business perk rather than a personal expense. A glimpse of his home, however, could not be so conveniently explained away. Clearly, Sev was wealthy, *very* wealthy. She preceded him into a wide, graciously furnished hall where he was greeted by an older woman from whom he ordered what he called 'supper'. She hoped it would be substantial because she needed food to ground her in surroundings in which she felt seriously out of her depth.

Harley trotted confidently into a contemporary drawing room where he leapt up onto a sofa. Sev said something and the dog slowly removed itself from the seat to drop down on a rug instead. 'He's not perfect yet,' Sev commented. 'But he's getting there. Take a seat.'

Sev lounged by the fireplace, looking impossibly gorgeous, and every time she glanced in that direction she could feel her face warming and her body heating to an uncomfortable degree. He offered her a drink, but she demurred, knowing she would fall asleep on him if she took alcohol on an empty stomach. It was a relief when the older woman bustled in with a tray heaped with snacks, and coffee followed, strong and stimulating, exactly what she needed to stay alert.

Harley shuffled over to her feet and nudged at her ankles, in search of both food and affection. Conscious that Sev was training him, she didn't give him any scraps, but she stretched a hand down to fondle his silky ears.

Sev watched her pour the coffee and extend

a cup and saucer to him and an overwhelming hunger filled him because she was so gentle with the dog. He had only ever seen that innate soothing tenderness in Annabel before and, if he was honest with himself, he had viewed it as a dangerous trait that would lead to her being hurt. And how right he'd been there!

'Aren't you hungry?' Amy asked, conscious that she had made serious inroads into the delicious snacks while he stood back, content with a coffee. 'I'm afraid that I have a very healthy appetite.'

'Nothing wrong with that. I ate earlier.' As Sev settled his empty cup down on the tray, the fine fabric of his trousers pulled across his lean muscular thighs and another surge of heat flashed through her. He had a beautiful body and the thought embarrassed her, but she had never been so aware of a man's physicality before, was shaken by the manner in which her attention was continually drawn to him. Sev simply radiated earthy sex appeal.

His phone rang and he pulled it out with a frown. 'Sorry, I need to take this...'

Her violet gaze clung to him as he walked restively across the spacious room, talking to someone he called Ethan, whom he was evidently surprised to hear from. The conversation swiftly grew abrupt because Sev was shooting anxious questions that made it clear that some woman was ill or had been hurt in some way. Anxiety stamping his lean, darkly handsome features, he said that he would be coming straight to the hospital.

In a rush, Amy stood up. 'Look, I'll head home. I gather you've got an emergency on your hands—'

Sev groaned out loud. 'No, you can come with me. I don't know how to handle this. That was a family friend. My sister is in hospital under observation. She fell and there's a chance that she could have a miscarriage.'

'Oh, my goodness, how ghastly! Why on earth would you want me to intrude?'

Pale below his olive skin, Sev settled glittering bronze eyes on her. 'Because I haven't a clue how to handle this but I suspect that you'll know exactly what to say. I don't want to hurt her feelings. Ethan says she's hysterical and that she needs to calm down. She does get a bit overwrought when her feelings are involved.'

'Who's Ethan?' Amy pressed.

'A family friend, a doctor. She phoned him for advice when she started bleeding and he took care of her admission but he's not in obstetrics. I've authorised him to get a consultant in so that we know what's happening.'

'From what I've heard there are no guarantees with a threatened miscarriage. You just have to wait and see,' Amy told him uncertainly.

'This is not how I expected this evening to go,' Sev murmured heavily. 'My apologies.'

CHAPTER FOUR

SEV'S SISTER HAD been admitted to a private hospital, a recently built commanding property glinting with glass and exclusivity and bristling with staff. They were greeted in the entrance foyer by a young dark-haired man who introduced himself as Dr Ethan Foster.

Amy quickly realised that he and Sev were old friends and that he was well acquainted with Sev's sister, Annabel, as well. Amy stood uncomfortably to one side, striving not to eavesdrop while Ethan brought Sev up to speed on events. There was a lot of low-voiced speech and she noticed Sev throwing his proud dark head up angrily at one point, even white teeth gritting as though he had learned something that outraged him. Just then, feeling very much surplus to requirements, Amy was tempted to kick Sev for dragging her along and she was determined not to even show her face near his poor sister, who would surely resent the appearance of a complete stranger at such a stressful time.

'What was all that about?' she whispered in the lift.

Sev dealt her a grim glance. 'I'll explain later but right now I need to stay calm for Annabel's benefit. She doesn't need me stalking in to tell her that she picked a bad guy. After what she's been through with him, she already knows that.'

As Sev strode into the private room from which she could hear the sound of sobbing, Amy stayed in the corridor and the doctor, Ethan, grimaced. 'Blame me for this. I didn't fully understand the situation and, of course, the first people I contacted were Annabel's parents and I let them speak to her on the phone, assuming that they would support her…but they're not supportive of her continuing the pregnancy and the last thing she needed was to be virtually congratulated on her potential loss!'

'Oh, heavens, no,' Amy agreed with a grimace. 'That must've made her feel worse. Sev's the only real support she has.'

'He's never been the emotional type. It will be a challenge for him to find the right words—' His voice broke off as a woman's raised voice emanated through the ajar door.

'You agree with them, don't you? Why don't you just *admit* it? You think if I lose this child, it'll be the best thing for everyone!' Annabel condemned shakily.

It was compassion for them both that prompted Amy to intervene because she knew that Sev didn't deserve that accusation and that he was deeply concerned about his sister.

'Now don't go making assumptions,' Amy murmured quietly as she entered the room. Ducking deftly past Sev, she moved down the side of the bed to look at the flushed blonde woman sitting up in it. She found it disorientating that, with her fair colouring and light blue eyes, Annabel bore not the smallest resemblance to her black-haired, dark-eyed big brother. 'Sev's worried sick about you and about your child.'

'Who the heck are you?' Annabel gasped in understandable bewilderment.

'Just a friend. My name's Amy.'

'Well, you can see how many friends I've got at the minute by the emptiness of this room,' Annabel breathed tartly. 'There probably isn't going to *be* a baby now though, so—'

'Wait for the scan, wait and see,' Amy urged in gentle interruption. 'Don't automatically assume the worst. It's much too soon for that.'

Sev watched in fascination as Amy talked his sister down from her emotional peak, using nothing more than her quiet voice, positive outlook and a sympathetic expression. Within a matter of minutes, Annabel had stopped actively crying and was anxiously sharing the story of events of earlier that evening, mentioning physical warning signs that made Sev squeamish and he would sooner not have heard, sending him in retreat to the door. In the midst of her story, Annabel suggested that Amy take a seat and asked if Sev could get them some tea.

'Decaf only,' she warned him. 'I'm being very careful.'

'Of course, you are,' Amy chipped in approvingly.

'Do you have a child?'

'No. At the moment a dog is my child substitute,' Amy admitted with a grin, telling Sev's sister about Hopper and Harley and then explaining that she had been with Sev when Ethan contacted him.

Annabel gave her a wondering appraisal. 'Don't be offended when I say that you're not my brother's usual type.'

'I didn't think so but I'm just seeing how it goes,' Amy admitted with calm acceptance.

Annabel explained that the father of her child didn't want her to have their child and that his attitude and the lies he had told had led to a bitter end to their relationship. In an effort to remedy that, Annabel had agreed to meet the man she called Olly earlier that evening at his request, but that meeting had quickly gone sour, ending in an argument and her sudden departure. In her haste to escape his verbal attacks she had slipped and tumbled down a couple of steps into the street. Amy listened, inputting an occasional word of empathy and, throughout, Annabel became less emotional and less tearful. It was after midnight by the time the consultant appeared, his friendly manner and practical opinion of the situation soothing his patient even more. By the time the scanning machine was wheeled in, Annabel was becoming sleepy. Amy offered to leave but Sev's sister reached out for her hand and urged her to stay with her.

As Amy moved out of the seat to leave space for the technician to operate, Sev smiled at her from the doorway and it was a dazzling smile that made her tummy flip and her knees weak. She went pink and hastily looked away again. Moments later as the scanner revealed the flashing heartbeat of her child Annabel beamed with joy and everyone else breathed a sigh of relief that, for the moment at least, tragedy had been averted.

'Time for us to go home,' Sev murmured after chatting to the consultant for a few minutes.

Amy screened a guilty yawn with her hand as they travelled down in the lift. 'You were very angry before you saw your sister,' she murmured uncertainly.

'Ethan explained what had happened this evening with the baby's father. That bastard has been harassing Annabel with calls. He persuaded her to meet up with him again. Of course, he turned nasty fast. She could have been seriously hurt… *Anything* could have happened!' he seethed.

'He sounds like a real piece of work.'

Sev gritted his teeth in frustrated rage, a feverish line of colour accentuating the hard line of his high cheekbones as he recalled Annabel's wan face and haunted eyes in that hospital bed. It would have given him the greatest of pleasure to visit Lawson and plant a fist in his smug, bullying face to punish him, but such open aggression would blow his plans, and revenge was a dish better eaten cold, he reminded himself grimly. He could not afford to reveal his family connection with Annabel until *after* he had attended the Lawson party because that invitation would be quickly withdrawn if his quarry realised who he was.

Noting the taut lines of his classic profile, Amy breathed in deeply as they crossed the car park to the limousine awaiting them. 'It's over now and she and the baby are safe,' she pointed out quietly.

'But they should *never* have been at risk in the first place!' he countered through gritted teeth of lingering anger. 'He *knows* she's pregnant. He should never have subjected her to a scene like that.'

Powerful emotion glinted in his eyes and it called to Amy like a log fire on a cold day. For all his cool sophistication, which if anything made Amy more wary of him, Sev was clearly a guy capable of deep, strong feeling and she was impressed by the strength of his attachment to his sister and his protectiveness. Sev, she acknowledged, wasn't quite what he might seem to be on his gilded and polished surface. He wasn't all show and gloss alone.

'No, they shouldn't have been at risk,' she agreed. 'But I assume you're planning to make sure it *doesn't* happen again.'

Sev jerked his chin down in a strong nod of confirmation, confident that after the party Lawson would be keen to stay well away from him and his sister, rather than risk further messy revelations in a social climate that admired good judgement and caution and punished the indiscreet. He urged Amy into the car, his keen gaze locked to the glow of admiration in her bright violet eyes. Hunger as fierce as a sudden storm gripped him in an overwhelming surge, arousal pulsing through his lean, powerful frame.

'*Stay* with me tonight,' Sev breathed in a

driven undertone, fiercely reluctant to part with her, wondering if it had been sharing his sister's unhappy experience with Amy that had made him feel closer to her.

CHAPTER FIVE

SURPRISE AND PLEASURE consumed Amy because she immediately believed that Sev had to be experiencing the same intense sense of connection that she was and for the very first time sexual intimacy struck her as the most natural next step in a relationship. Her face flushed as a wave of heat ran through her entire body and he bent his head down and kissed her.

Exhilaration tugged at the very core of her, making her slender thighs tremble. Her lips clung to his until the ragged breath he drew in after that first kiss fanned her cheek. He lifted his dark head, his brilliant gaze glittering like stardust in a night sky. 'I want you so much I ache, *mia piccola.*'

And to hell with all common sense and restraint, Sev thought rawly. Sex would be no big deal for her. Why would it be? Why was he making such a heavy production out of following his natural instincts? She wanted him as much as he wanted her! His shrewd brain well aware that he was talking himself into what he was unaccountably desperate to do, he tasted the ripe sweetness of her peachy lips and lost himself in her honey-sweet response. For such a very small package, he acknowledged, she packed one hell of a punch in the passion stakes, because he didn't think he had *ever* been so aroused.

Amy had never experienced passion of that nature, kisses that burned and just weren't *enough*, the firm stroke of masculine hands over her still-clothed figure inspiring a startling spasm of frustration that he was *not* actually touching her bare skin. The feverish rush of sensation blew her every clear thought into outer space because she had never dreamt, never even hoped, that any guy could make her feel anything as strongly as Sev did. It was mutual: it felt...*right*. Her heart was pounding inside her chest, her pulses racing.

'Yes,' she heard herself say with unusual confidence. 'Yes, I'll stay.' And after she had spoken, she could barely believe she had made that decision.

It wasn't as though she had been saving her virginity for marriage, she reasoned, it was only that she had been waiting for someone who made her feel special, and Sev *did*. There was so much she liked about him as well: his having given a rescue animal a good home, his loving, caring support of his sister, his complete indifference to her social standing and income level in comparison to his own. All those traits had huge appeal for Amy and made him almost a perfect specimen of true masculinity in her eyes.

Sev closed a taut arm round her slight figure and drew her close, breathing in slow and deep in relief to steady himself. His zip was biting into his arousal. He was the closest he had ever been, or ever even *thought* to be, to having sex in his limo. Tacky, grubby, he censured himself, incredulous at that powerful prompting that had come at him out of nowhere like one of those stupid ideas that occurred to a horny teenager, *not* an adult male. Amy was coming home with him for the night and he could relax…

Amy settled into the reassuring warmth of his embrace and struggled to settle her over-anxious brain, which was still shooting thoughts at her at an almost hysterical speed because Amy didn't usually make hasty decisions about anyone or anything. Having to be more independent from an early age had made her cautious and careful beyond her years. But in her heart of hearts, where she had never had reason to probe before, she *knew* that she was falling in love with Sev, with a man whose surname she couldn't even spell, she scolded herself ruefully. The strength of her feelings unnerved her a little but she was determined not to be a scaredy-cat, protecting herself from imagined dangers even when she saw no just cause to behave that way: Sev had somehow taught her to trust him at a very early stage and she didn't question that gut instinct.

Long fingers tilted up her chin. She gazed up into dark golden eyes that melted her to liquid honey. He closed his mouth over hers again and she quivered, her entire body lighting up as he tasted her, worrying at her lower lip with the blunt edge of his teeth, teasing and awakening with the ravishing plunge of his tongue. It was wildly arousing and wildly frustrating at the same time and she was in a daze by the time he tugged her out of the car.

The next thing she knew, she was in the dimly lit hall and Sev was urging her back against a wall and claiming her swollen mouth again. It was electrifying, the pulse between her slender thighs rising to a dulled insistent ache that was maddening.

'*Dio…*you burn me up,' Sev growled, reaching down to lift her legs and push between them, that sudden physical connection striking her like a red-hot coal as his lean, muscular body pressed against the humming heat at the heart of her.

In an equally sudden movement, he bent and swept her off her feet into his arms, startling her. 'You can't carry me!' she gasped in consternation.

'Of course, I can.' Sev laughed as he mounted the stairs with ease. 'You're tiny and you weigh next to nothing. Maybe I've been waiting all my adult life for a woman I can carry around as easily as a parcel!'

'I wouldn't say you're very good at waiting for anything,' Amy mumbled, yet she was somehow humbled by the obvious truth that he was as eager for her as she was for him. It had to be one of those weird sexual-attraction conundrums because she still could not quite believe that a man as hot and beautiful as Sev could feel the same about her as she did about him. It was a miracle, she thought in a daze, a wonderful, magical development in a life that had inured her more to disappointments than rewards.

Magical, she was still reckoning as he tumbled her down on a massive bed in a huge, beautifully decorated room. As he dimmed the lights she scanned her surroundings with appreciation, admiring the subtle colour scheme, the silken folds of the drapes and the plain contemporary furniture, but she was also a little intimidated by that reminder of what vastly different worlds they inhabited... For goodness' sake, she lived in a converted storeroom and cooked on a one-ring mini oven! Her world was workaday and ordinary and just paying the bills was a struggle. His world was utterly alien to her own. She wasn't foolish enough to assume that his wealth automatically gave him a carefree existence, but she was very much aware that she really had no idea how his life operated. And that bothered her because she wanted to understand everything about Sev, indeed was experiencing an almost obsessional need to learn every tiny detail there was to know.

'All of a sudden you look so deadly serious and worried,' Sev remarked, his shrewd scrutiny noting the tension etched in her delicate features. She was so beautiful he couldn't take his eyes off her. He marvelled that he had ever believed that he would be able to resist her allure, but then such an irresistible attraction to a woman was absolutely new to him and all the more exciting for that, he acknowledged, peeling off his jacket and casting it aside before bending down to flip off her canvas shoes and tug off her socks, exposing tiny feet.

A little unnerved by that bold approach, Amy sat up. 'I'm not worried about anything,' she lied, because she wasn't prepared to tell him that he was going to be her first lover. He might find that prospect a turn-off, might even think her immature because most women her age had experimented more than she had. But yes, she was nervous, horribly self-conscious and afraid of making a wrong move of some kind. Trying to fake cool and casual didn't come easily to her.

'You're still wearing too many clothes,' Sev purred, coming down on the bed to run down the zip on her jeans and then vaulting off again to tug her jeans off.

Amy shivered, suddenly cold in the warm room, feeling the goose bumps of nerves rise all over her exposed skin. One knee on the bed, Sev closed his hands round her narrow ribcage and lifted her up to him to kiss her again, tasting her soft lips with unalloyed hunger. A little sound escaped from low in her throat and it drove his excitement even higher. He eased off her sweater with more care than he felt like utilising, struggling to get a grip on his control. Her breasts were plump, luscious swells in lace-edged cups and he snatched in a ragged breath, leaning back from her to tear his shirt off.

Lean muscles rippled as he moved, exposing a sculpted chest worthy of a men's health magazine, and the earthy, musky and masculine scent of him assailed her nostrils. He smelled so incredibly good that she wanted to bury her nose in him, and she flushed, suddenly achingly vulnerable, her eyes locking anxiously to his.

'You have the most amazing eyes, *piccolo mia*,' he growled and her bra fell away, allowing his hands to rise up and cup the full firm mounds, his thumbs rubbing over the straining pink nipples, provoking a gasp from her parted lips. 'But why do you look so scared?'

'I'm not scared!' Amy parried. 'Where did you get that idea?'

Beneath his palm her heart was racing like a trapped bird's. He pressed her back against the pillows and closed his mouth hungrily to a pouting nipple, sucking on the tender tip until her spine came up off the bed and she squirmed. It felt as if a hot wire were tightening inside her pelvis, she thought dizzily, sending every pulse in her trembling body onto high alert. Long fingers smoothed up her inner thigh.

'Your skin feels like silk,' Sev groaned, struggling out of what remained of his clothes while he explored her tender breasts with his mouth and she writhed beneath him, her response sending his raging arousal even higher.

All of a sudden, nothing mattered to Sev but getting inside her, sating that overwhelming hunger driving him. He tugged away the last barrier between them, discovering that she was wet and ready for him, but at the last minute he reminded himself that he specialised in being a slow, unselfish lover. He shimmied down the bed and spread her slender thighs, licking the tender entrance he couldn't wait to breach.

A deluge of sensation engulfed Amy at the same time as she couldn't credit what he was doing. Her innate shyness fought with the demands of her needy body. For a moment she believed she would stop him and then, the next moment, nothing on earth could have persuaded her to stop him. Exquisite sensation such as she had never felt claimed her, entrapped her, transformed her into a thrashing frenzy of naked want. As sensation piled on sensation and the pleasure became unbearable, the tightness in her pelvis suddenly mushroomed up inside her into an explosive climax that left her seeing stars.

Sev shifted over her, lithe as a jungle cat in his urgency. He hauled her up under him and drove deep into her tight body with a heartfelt groan of relief. A piercing sharp pain broke through Amy's idyllic state and she gritted her teeth against a broad brown shoulder, praying for the pain to fade. And it did, petering out into a vague discomfort that was soon beyond her awareness as Sev's movements and the newness of the experience took precedence.

Her body had stretched to accommodate him and the slight burn of his plunging thrusts and subsequent withdrawal was an incredibly arousing experience. Surprised that her body was so willing to find pleasure again, she discovered that his rhythm excited her unbearably. The hungry ache at the heart of her began to grow in strength again, her hips rising, her heart pumping. All of a sudden her whole being was concentrated on the churning excitement consuming her and she was reaching…and reaching higher and higher, craving that ultimate climax until it came in a storm of consuming sensation.

She fell back limp on the bed, absolutely drained.

Beside her, Sev went from sated to incredulous at the discovery that he had not used a condom. 'I forgot to use contraception...' he breathed rawly. 'I don't know what came over me. I've never done that before.'

Jolted by that confession, Amy shifted, however, with a faint smile of relief that she had protected herself from the risk of an unplanned pregnancy. 'Relax, I'm on the pill. Nothing's going to happen.'

'I've never had sex without contraception before so you're safe,' Sev bit out, still deeply shaken by his own carelessness.

'And you're safe because I've never been with anyone else,' Amy whispered, still struggling to return to her normal thought processes.

Without warning, Sev sat up. *'Never?'* he queried in astonishment.

Amy winced because she had originally intended to keep that fact to herself and so she didn't answer, she simply compressed her lips.

'You were a virgin?' Sev pressed more harshly.

'Everybody has to have a first at some stage of their lives,' she muttered ruefully. 'Please don't embarrass me by making a production out of it.'

Sev released his breath in a slow controlled huff of sound, swallowing back his annoyance and frustration that she hadn't warned him in advance. He was in no mood to preach, though, when he himself had just made his worst ever mistake in neglecting to take precautions with a woman. 'Fancy a shower?' he murmured lightly, keen to change the subject.

'I think it's time I went home, got a shower there,' Amy told him in a sudden decision, reacting to the tension in the air.

'I want you to stay the night,' Sev confided, faint colour scoring his high cheekbones because for the first time in his life he was inviting a woman to stay over. He never ever did that. Indeed, he usually went to the woman's place or a hotel, not his own home, which he preferred to keep strictly private. It bothered him that he didn't know why he was inviting Amy any more than he recognised his deep visceral need to keep her close. But he suppressed those uneasy reactions, refused even to think about the fact she had been a virgin, and instead he focused on the truth that he had just had the best sex of his life and *obviously* he wanted to hold on to her, the promise of pleasure being the ultimate seducer.

'Still?' Amy queried, hugging the duvet.

'Still,' Sev stressed without hesitation, closing an arm round her and pulling her close to kiss her again. 'I also want to talk to you about a party I'd like you to attend with me next week.'

'A party?' Amy repeated, wide-eyed, snuggling into him with a feeling of warmth and security that was new to her. She had expected him to be cooler in the aftermath of sex, not anchoring her to him and insisting she stay, and the reference to a further date could only make her smile. 'I'd love to come.'

'But there's one proviso. It's a very fancy party and you'll have to let me buy you a dress for the occasion.'

Her violet gaze widened in dismay. 'Oh, I couldn't agree to that.'

'You can't go, then, which would be a shame,' Sev murmured, pinning her under him as he flipped over, his breath fanning her cheek. 'One little outfit…that's all. You wouldn't be able to *borrow* anything appropriate.'

Her heart pounding at his proximity and the intimacy of his embrace, Amy stared up into liquid-bronze eyes framed by thick black lashes, so very beautiful. 'But it wouldn't feel right letting you pay for it.'

'I'll make it feel right,' Sev intoned.

'You can hire dresses these days!' Amy croaked as he kneed her thighs apart and slid fluidly between them again.

'No way are we *hiring* a dress. I'll make an appointment for you with a stylist I know…

OK?' Sev prompted, shifting his renewed arousal against the most sensitive part of her entire body and sending a cascade of awakening sensation through her again.

'OK,' she muttered breathlessly.

His mouth teased at the edge of hers again and her body clenched deep inside, both the scent and the touch of him a source of wild excitement. 'I still want you... You're not a hunger easily assuaged... Do you think you could bear a repeat encounter? Or is it too soon?'

'Yes...*yes*...no, it's not too soon,' Amy framed in a happy rush, wrapping her arms round him, fingers spearing into his tousled black hair with an intimacy she would not have dared employ with him earlier that evening, but then everything between them had changed irrevocably, she acknowledged without regret. She felt much closer to him than she had, and she was glad that she had taken a leap in the dark and decided to trust him and her own feelings.

CHAPTER SIX

GEMMA SNAPPED PHOTO after photo of Amy as soon as she was all dressed up for the party. 'I'm not joking. You look absolutely gorgeous!' the redhead enthused, having offered to come over to do Amy's make-up for her and do up the hooks on her gown. 'That dress is to die for!'

Amy winced. 'I'm still wondering what it all cost. Nothing was priced at that place. There wasn't a single price tag on anything I saw.'

'What does it matter?' Gemma laughed. 'By the sound of it, this guy has plenty of money. If he wants to take you to some superfancy party, why shouldn't he help out?'

Amy nodded, striving to emulate her friend's down-to-earth take on the situation. She kicked out a toe to take yet another appreciative look at the glistening dark purple and diamanté finish on her high heels. 'Every girl should get to play Cinderella for a night just once,' she agreed, breathing in deep and anxiously glancing down to check the swell of cleavage that the corset top of the dress exposed. 'You don't think it's too revealing?'

'No, I don't. If you've got it, flaunt it! I love the colour the most…it's really different.'

'Yes, I was expecting to be fitted out with a designer little black dress, not something magical like this…' The delicate full skirts swishing round her ankles, Amy studied the deep violet hue of the shimmering fabric below the lights. 'Since Sev's paying for it, I hope he likes it.'

'Don't forget the evening coat…' Gemma sighed enviously, shaking out the silky garment and extending it. 'A coat that matches and then the shoes and that adorable little clutch bag. It's just the most amazing outfit… People will notice you.'

Amy winced. 'I don't want to be noticed by anyone but Sev.'

For an entire week she had thought of nothing but the night she had spent in Sev's arms. It had been a night of passion such as she had never expected to experience, a revolutionary encounter with a sensual self she had not even known existed. In the aftermath she had been shocked by how much she had enjoyed sex. Well, sex with Sev, at least, she adjusted, her face burning. Every time he had touched her that night, she had succumbed. A couple of days afterwards Sev had invited her to an art showing but she had already had to ask Harold for an evening off to go to the party and it would have been too much for her to ask for a second, so she had had to decline with regret, which meant she hadn't seen Sev since that night.

Even so, he had phoned her several times, ensuring that she didn't feel neglected or forgotten. There had been little chats about nothing in particular that she treasured, chats that had centred on daily events at the surgery or on Harley. It hadn't got much more personal than that from his side and that continuing reserve of his had bothered her. The closest they had got to personal was when she had asked how his sister was doing. Apparently, Annabel had made a good recovery and was returning to work, but no further information had been offered.

Sadly, Amy had waited in vain for Sev to invite her over after the surgery had closed in the evening. She wouldn't have objected to intimacy without a date attached, because she was the one unavailable and she missed him, but he hadn't made that move and Amy didn't want to seem pushy or off-puttingly keen, and so she hadn't made that suggestion. What that meant was that she was rather more nervous about the evening ahead and already wondering if Sev was regretting inviting her to accompany him. Or was she being paranoid? Imagining the new worrying distance she had sensed in his voice during his calls?

* * *

A couple more hours and it would all be over, Sev thought with relief as he swung into his limo to pick up Amy. Annabel would be avenged, and Amy would walk away with a diamond necklace worth a king's ransom and the knowledge of her paternity that she should always have had. It would be a fitting conclusion to an unpleasant business. And at the end of the night they would *celebrate together*, he reflected with a slashing smile of satisfaction, thinking that just for once he might not be so quick to ditch a woman to seek the next because Amy had proved to be something else. A something else that Sev had never come across before: a woman who looked for nothing from him other than himself. She had made such a fuss about accepting that one stupid dress and she was forever asking him about the kind of stuff he never discussed with anyone, hungry for *him* though, not hungry for what he could *give* her...except in bed. And between the sheets Amy had been even more of a revelation. Innocent but sensual, an untaught but absolutely instinctive lover.

He still could not quite credit that a virgin had given him the best sex of his life, and discovering that he was the only lover she had ever had had proved surprisingly arousing as well. He had gone from guilty unease over that unexpected bombshell to the acceptance that they were both adults who had relished the encounter. *Dio*…he had enjoyed that night and her over and over again and staying away from her all week had been a serious challenge for his libido. Thankfully, however, common sense had kicked in and restrained him from giving way to temptation. First of all, he had had to prove to his own satisfaction that he *could* stay away from her if he chose to do so. And of course, he didn't want to give Amy the wrong message either. He didn't want her to start thinking that their little fling had a future, because of course it didn't, he reasoned wryly. Inevitably he would, *eventually*, get bored and move on.

Amy stepped out onto the street and moved towards the limousine with an uncertain smile. For several disturbing seconds Sev couldn't take his eyes off her. He had specified violet for the dress, described exactly what he wanted and paid a premium price for that luxury and the reward was the reality that Amy looked as ravishing as a fairy princess, the subdued glitter of the gown enhancing the natural glow of her porcelain-fine skin and her brilliant eyes, the delicate drape of the fine fabric shaping her tiny slender frame, framing an impossibly small waist and the soft pale swell of her breasts rising from the lace-edged bodice. He went instantly hard as she climbed into the limo, a waft of subtle fragrance accompanying her as she settled onto the seat beside him.

She met eyes set beneath black brows and it was as if a shot of live electricity sizzled through her body. Her palms went damp and her tummy lurched, a giddy exhilaration momentarily gripping her. With difficulty she clasped her trembling hands together on her lap while she told herself to calm down.

'I have a gift for you,' Sev murmured, sliding an oblong shallow case off the seat and laying it on her lap.

Amy frowned. 'But why? I mean, it's not my birthday or anything.'

'No, it's not your birthday until next month,' Sev told her, startling her with his knowledge of that date, because she could not recall either him asking or her telling him when her birthday was. 'But I thought you might like to wear this tonight.'

Her heart sank at the suggestion that what looked like a jewellery box was truly one because accepting the dress and accessories had been a big enough stretch of what she thought was right and decent in a relationship. Her fingers flipped open the case and a river of diamonds shone as the streetlights outside illuminated the jewels with rainbow fire. 'Oh, my goodness, I couldn't accept something like this!' she gasped in dismay.

'Let me...' Long brown fingers deftly detached the necklace from the case and touched her shoulder to turn her round. 'Try it on.'

'But I don't want to,' she told him uncomfortably. 'I can't possibly let you give me something so valuable.'

Cool metal rested against her skin and she shivered, recalling his hands gliding over her sensitive skin that night. *'Sev...'*

'Maybe it's fake?'

She pressed cool fingers to the item. 'Is it?' she asked hopefully.

'No, it's not. Make use of it this evening, see how you feel then,' Sev suggested coolly. 'You don't own any jewels. I simply thought you would feel less bare wearing something.'

Unnerved by that cool tone and afraid that she had offended him, Amy paled, mentally scrabbling for something soothing to say. 'It's not that I'm not grateful...it's just too much. We haven't known each other very long.'

'I was worried that you would feel self-conscious tonight without jewellery.'

Amy swallowed hard. 'Look, I'll wear it for the evening and then return it to you, if that's all right. Thank you very much.'

'It's just a token,' Sev said dismissively, coiling back into the corner.

Amy patted the necklace uncomfortably and dropped her hand uneasily again. A… *token*? A *diamond* necklace? She would've preferred to take it off again but there was a cool light in those stunning dark golden eyes of his and it made her wary. She would wear it for the evening and return it afterwards, she told herself. Sev was in the strangest mood, she acknowledged worriedly, wondering if he had had a bad day, a bad week, whatever, but she was reassured by the near sizzle that lit the air when their eyes collided. As the limo drew up at the airport, she froze in surprise.

'We're using a helicopter to get to the party,' Sev explained as she looked at him in bewilderment. 'I don't like long drives and it would be an even longer drive home.'

'Oh…' she mumbled, climbing out into

what felt like a phalanx of overprotective men as Sev's security team converged to escort them into and through the airport at speed.

'Where's the party being held?' she asked, breathlessly trying to keep up with Sev's long, fluid stride. He was so tall as well, and looked even taller in the tailored black dinner jacket and long tailored trousers he wore.

'A country house in Norfolk. Our hosts are Oliver and Cecily Lawson. He's a businessman,' Sev imparted almost curtly as a door into the VIP lounge was held wide for their entrance. 'It's a fancy-dress party but I don't *do* fancy dress.'

'Fancy dress?' she repeated with a frown. 'But why don't you do it?'

'My mother is also very fond of costume parties,' Sev revealed with a biting edge to his dark drawl as they stood in the almost empty VIP room. 'She dressed me up as a cartoon character when I was eight and I was groped by a pervert at one of her parties. So, I don't do fancy dress any more.'

Amy stared up at him aghast, her attention locked to the carved perfect symmetry of his lean, darkly handsome features. 'A pervert?'

'A powerful politician…long dead now,' he extended grudgingly between clenched teeth. 'You look amazing, by the way, and there are very few, if any, women who could still look amazing under lights as bright as these.'

The abrupt change of subject startled her. 'Thank you, but I'm more interested in what happened to the man *after* he—'

Sev elevated a cynical brow. '*Nothing* happened to him. My mother slapped my face and accused me of lying and I was sent back to school in disgrace.'

'Oh, my goodness, Sev…what sort of a mother is she?' she whispered in horror.

'Not a caring one. Annabel is the only gold to be found in the dross of the Aiken clan,' he told her grimly. 'My father's relatives are completely normal though.'

Only Amy remembered him telling her that he hadn't got to know his father until he had grown up and all she could think then with pained compassion was that he must have been a very unhappy child. Her hand sought out his in a consoling squeeze that utterly took him aback, shocked dark eyes glittering down at her. 'I'm so sorry you had to go through that experience without help...'

Sev saw actual tears of sympathy glistening in her extraordinary violet eyes and his lush black lashes fluttered down for a split second while he inwardly cursed his attack of oversharing and her extraordinary empathy. What the hell was the matter with him? Why did the barriers come down and the secrets come flooding out only with her? What was it about *her*? The way she looked at him? The softness of that breathy little voice or those incredible eyes? Why the hell had he told her about that frightening incident? Something that, after his mother's reaction, he had never told to another living soul?

'So, won't we look odd not wearing fancy dress at the party?' Amy prompted, considerate enough to recognise when a subject needed to be changed.

'No, I'm rich enough to be forgiven for my idiosyncrasies and you could be dressed up as a fairy-tale princess in that gown. I did consider ordering a mask for you, but I didn't want that beautiful face of yours hidden,' Sev admitted, a little of the tension escaping his tall muscular frame.

He wanted the evening over, Oliver Lawson done and dusted and buried, staked like a vampire by his rich wife's discovery that her husband had a secret daughter conceived *after* his marriage. That desired objective achieved, he could forget about Lawson. His civilised revenge would be complete. Cecily Lawson was no fool and she would mete out her own punishment. Sev could do nothing more because he was not prepared to expose his sister's former relationship with Cecily's husband.

After it was done, he would take Amy home with him, fill her in on her background and *tie* her to his bed so that she couldn't go back to work, because she worked way too many hours. He had never met a woman so unavailable and she was straight as a ruler as well, wouldn't even *consider* lying and calling in sick to be with him, because he *had* suggested that option after their one and only night together. Amy would give him his downtime, his relaxation. She would be his reward for not smashing Lawson's teeth down his throat like a caveman.

They landed in a rough paddock and Sev lifted her out, carrying her over to the neatly mown path that led towards the big brilliantly lit house ahead. There were other helicopters sitting parked and a vast array of luxury cars fronting the building as well. Amy breathed in deep, terrified that in some way she might let Sev down by saying or doing the wrong thing. She would keep quiet, concentrate on being a good listener, she told herself, because letting Sev down in public when he had been so kind to her wasn't a possibility she could bear to entertain.

He paused for a moment on the path, gazing down at her before he lifted her up to him and kissed her breathless, crushing her lips under his, plunging his tongue into the moist interior of her mouth, sending a fizzing, desperate energy tunnelling through every skin cell. 'You taste so good,' he growled, setting her down again like a doll.

'I've probably covered you in lip gloss,' she warned him shakily.

'It was worth it,' he said, wiping his mouth and angling a slashing smile down at her that made her burn.

His hand welded to her spine, he ushered her into the house where a maid whisked away her evening coat and another proffered champagne. Sev steered her through the chattering groups with ease, pausing now and then to speak to someone who hailed him, briefly introducing her before moving on into a ballroom where several couples were already dancing.

'I think some people mistook the Christmas theme for Halloween,' she whispered with amusement, watching a man in a neon skeleton suit twirl while his partner, dressed as a ghost, pranced around him. Here and there she saw one or two other people, who hadn't bothered to dress up, but they had chosen to wear masks.

A flashy brunette sporting a sort of fantasy jungle outfit that exposed ninety per cent of her perfect body swam up to them and draped herself with frank familiarity over Sev as if Amy were invisible. She whispered something in his ear, giggled and studied him with lascivious heat in her dark gaze. He said something brief, shrugging her off like an annoying mosquito, and walked on. They joined a crowd who were already seated round a table and Sev was relentlessly teased for not having worn a costume or mask. He took it in good part. The men talked about business while the women chatted about holidays, children and fashion.

'Sorry, I'm not asking anything about you,' the woman beside her remarked, after Amy had sat listening to her talk wittily about her villa vacation in Italy. 'I think it's because we never see Sev with the same woman twice and it seems like a waste of time making the effort to get to know his partners.'

It was an eye-opening comment and not accidental either, for Amy recognised the gleam of malice in the other woman's appraisal. It had been said to let her know that she wasn't anything special in Sev's life but, since Amy had always had a modest opinion of herself, the arrow of spite missed its target.

'I suppose you're a model or an actress or something,' the woman continued in a tone of boredom.

'Or something,' Amy responded, grasping Sev's hand with a smile as he extended it down to her to walk her in the direction of the buffet.

'I thought you looked in need of rescue,' Sev murmured as he passed her a plate. 'Eliza can be a bit of a shrew with other women.'

'She supposed that I was a model or an actress—'

'A *model* with your height?' Sev teased, gazing down at her with glittering dark golden eyes that made her heart pound like crazy inside her chest.

'I could be a hand or foot model!' Amy proclaimed, tilting her head back, long golden hair rippling across her shoulders as she lifted her chin. 'I had this horrific urge to say I was a hired escort just to shock her—'

Sev's gaze narrowed in surprise and wonderment. 'And bang would go my reputation with women!'

Amy wrinkled her small nose. 'But I know better and I'm not sure I would have had the nerve. My mother was like Eliza. If you dared to answer her back, she bit your head off,' she recalled ruefully. 'I learned young to mind my tongue. It was only when I was older that I dared to stand up to her.'

'It's amazing that with that upbringing you didn't turn into a bad-tempered witch as well,' Sev remarked as he looked down at her with unhidden appreciation and smiled.

And that smile of his, that note of open admiration in his dark deep voice, set Amy on fire with happiness and she marvelled at how close she felt to him in that moment.

'There are our hosts,' Sev murmured in a quiet aside.

Amy glanced at the couple, regally dressed as a medieval king and queen with crowns of holly. The man was blond and looked younger than the woman, who wore a silvery-grey bob with panache. 'They certainly know how to throw a good party,' she commented.

Sev picked an unoccupied table. They were about to sit down when the Lawsons approached them, the older couple wreathed in smiles of welcome.

'I'm so glad you were able to come this year, Sev.' Cecily Lawson beamed. 'I know how busy your social schedule must be.'

Her husband stretched out a hand to Amy. 'I'm Oliver…and you are?'

But before she could part her lips, Sev had stepped in to say, 'This is Amy Taylor, and I'm not quite sure what the etiquette is for introducing a father to a daughter?'

'A...*daughter*?' Cecily queried with a frown of disbelief, her husband echoing her query.

'Yes, Amy is Oliver's daughter...not that he's ever acknowledged her,' Sev completed smoothly.

'What age are you, my dear?' the older woman demanded.

'Twenty-three next month,' Sev supplied.

Amy's tongue was glued to the roof of her mouth by shock. She could feel her knees knocking together beneath her gown while the blood drained from her face and the whole time she was staring at Oliver Lawson with wide disbelieving eyes. Her brain was refusing to function, but she did notice that his hair was the same shade as hers and his eyes the same dark blue. At the same time, he just didn't look quite old enough to have a daughter her age because she would have assumed he was no more than forty.

'Do have a lovely evening,' Oliver's wife said stiffly, as pale as Amy as she turned to walk away. *'Oliver!'* she added sharply as her husband remained frozen to the same spot.

'I'm Annabel Aiken's half-brother,' Sev added in a low voice as the older man turned almost clumsily away and his head jerked back, his face white with shock, eyes stunned and appalled by that revelation as he finally grasped the connection that had led to his downfall.

Nervous perspiration was breaking out on Amy's clammy skin as the couple disappeared back into the crush.

'I've accomplished what I came here to do,' Sev told her unapologetically. 'We'll head home now.'

He gathered up the clutch bag Amy had laid down on the table, tucked it between her nerveless fingers and ushered her through the crowds back out to the foyer where he spoke briefly into his phone and asked a maid to fetch her evening coat for her.

Amy was feeling dizzy, shock still winging through her in wave after wave as she recalled Oliver Lawson's dead empty stare and the flash of distaste that had momentarily twisted his lips when her identity was laid bare. *Her father?* Was that even possible and how could Sev feasibly know who her father was and speak with such authority on the subject?

'I'll answer all your questions once we get back home,' Sev informed her quietly as he neatly threaded her stiff arms into her coat.

'What you did was...very bad manners,' she heard herself mumble pathetically for want of anything else to say because she was so desperately confused and shaken that she still felt sick.

'That's the least of my worries,' Sev told her bracingly, hand splaying in a supportive brace to her spine as he guided her out into the cold wintry air. 'Well, are you pleased to finally find out who your father is? Or disappointed that I found out first?'

'You knew who I was when you brought me here tonight,' Amy grasped belatedly, stricken to the heart by that obvious fact.

'We would never have met had I not found out who you were,' Sev admitted in a curt undertone. 'I know you won't like hearing that, but I refuse to lie to you any longer. What I never counted on was being knocked for six the first time I laid eyes on you. That wasn't supposed to happen but, now that I know you, I'm not sorry it did. I want you more than I've ever wanted a woman and even the fact that you're that lying bastard's daughter doesn't change that!'

Amy felt like a zombie because her brain felt as though it were drowning in sludge. She let Sev walk her out and lift her into the helicopter and she said nothing. He had detonated a bomb inside her head, and she wanted to scream because all of a sudden she was seeing that she had made a cartload of innocent assumptions about Sev and that every one of those assumptions was hopelessly wrong. Naturally she had believed that he was a stranger when they met, but that had not been the case when he had already known who she was.

Apparently, he had deliberately sought her out to use her for some nefarious purpose of his own. The noisy racket of the helicopter combined with the turmoil in her brain in a deafening cacophony.

Her identity as Oliver Lawson's secret daughter was the sole reason he had invited her to the party, heck, very probably the sole reason he had *ever* taken the smallest interest in her! Deeper shock engulfed her with sudden sharp emotional pain, all her secret dreams and fancies laid bare and smashed to smithereens. The helicopter flew back to London while Amy struggled to get a grip on herself because, while everything between her and Sev was now finished, she *did* want answers… At the very least she deserved that in recompense for the nasty little scene he had plunged her into at the party without her consent. If she had had to be a dupe, let her at least be a well-informed one, she told herself fiercely, refusing to give way to the biting hurt over his duplicity that was seething inside her… Sev didn't *care* about her at all, didn't care that he had hurt and humiliated her and betrayed her trust.

CHAPTER SEVEN

'IS IT TRUE? *Is* that man my father?' Amy asked sharply as the limo ferried them away from the airport. It was the first time she had been able to speak and expect to be heard since they had left the party and it was also the first moment that was truly private. The helicopter had been too noisy, and they had not been alone.

'It's true. I had Lawson investigated. Your mother worked in the same company with him for several years. He was actually engaged to her and living with her when the boss's daughter began to show an interest in him. He ditched your mother and married Cecily not long afterwards,' he explained curtly. 'His affair with your mother started up again after the marriage and that was when you were conceived. He's an ambitious man and marrying Cecily paid off handsomely. As soon as Cecily's father died, he became CEO of her family insurance firm.'

'It's extremely weird to get those facts from you, facts I would have liked to have known years ago but which my mother refused to share.' After making that honest admission, Amy released her breath audibly. 'What I still don't understand is what you have against Oliver Lawson that you would confront him like that with me tonight?'

Sev's spectacular bone structure tensed, his dark golden eyes shimmering with sudden aggression as he sent her a cool flashing glance. 'He's also the father of *Annabel's* baby.'

Further shock rippled through Amy and she froze then, her muscles bunching so tight that she ached all over. Oliver... *Olly*, she recalled his sister saying. More bad news, she thought unhappily, as if she did not already have enough to deal with, but there was the deeper, more personal motivation that had driven Sev. Unasked, he filled in the parts of his sibling's story that Amy hadn't known, and her heart sank even more. Her birth father, it seemed, was a total creep, a user and abuser of women, shallow, manipulative and dishonest and a complete bully when things didn't go his way. Two decades on, the man who had embittered and disillusioned her mother had clearly not changed for the better.

'I was determined to punish him but I also needed to protect my sister from further exposure,' Sev continued flatly. 'Once I found out about you and understood how very careful he had been to keep your existence a secret from his wife, I realised that you were his weakness and would make the perfect weapon.'

'The perfect pawn,' Amy contradicted bitterly, and then she compressed her lips together to prevent her emotional turmoil from spilling out and humiliating her even more. She was nobody, she was nothing to Sev, a means to an end and nasty Oliver's unwanted daughter. Sev had utilised her without any thought or consideration of what he might be doing to her. It hadn't mattered to him that in targeting her father and using her to do so, he would also be hurting her.

Amy clenched her teeth together so hard that her gums hurt as well. Like a robot, she got out of the car and preceded Sev into his home.

'I don't know about you, but I could do with a drink,' Sev confided.

'Water for me,' she said woodenly, incredulous at his unswerving composure, his entire attitude after what he had done to her.

'Take your coat off,' Sev urged.

'No…it's cool in here,' she fibbed, because she wasn't staying once she had told him what she thought of him. And that awareness reminded her of the diamond necklace she still wore, and she reached up under her hair to undo the clasp.

'What are you doing?' Sev asked.

'Taking it off. I wore it to be polite and I don't want to keep it,' she admitted curtly, detaching the necklace and laying it down on the nearest surface where it glittered accusingly at her. She hadn't wanted to accept or wear the wretched thing, but she had trampled over her own sense of morality to wear it simply to please Sev. Now that lowering recollection made her feel nauseous.

'I realise that all this has come out of nowhere at you and shaken you up,' Sev conceded, slotting a moisture-beaded glass into her hand. 'But I was hoping that you'd be pleased to finally find out your father's identity.'

'Oh, yes, so much to celebrate there!' Amy scorned in a voice that emerged with a shrill edge and didn't sound familiar even to her own ears. 'A father who is a lying, cheating adulterer! How am I supposed to feel about that discovery?'

'That's your private business,' Sev countered, watching her warily, seeing the colour now freshly highlighting her cheeks, the overbright sparkle of her violet eyes, finally recognising the fierce anger he had never seen in her before.

'Private?' Amy stressed. 'My goodness,

that's a funny word to use! As far as you're concerned, there's nothing private about my sad little life. You know more about my background and parentage than I do! And even worse, you knew it all even *before* I first met you, didn't you?'

Sev gritted his teeth, his strong jawline clenching. 'Yes. I didn't enjoy faking ignorance though. I'm relieved that I can be honest with you now.'

Amy drank down a gulp of sparkling water, her throat tight, her fingers even tighter on the glass because she wanted to throw it at him and was only just resisting the urge. He had made her feel like a fool and she didn't need to make that obvious by attacking him. 'But the damage is done, isn't it? You hate my father but you decided to punish *me*.'

'That's not true, Amy.'

'You mean you don't think it's a punishment for a woman to discover that the very first man she slept with was simply *using* her and playing her like a fish on a line?'

Sev shot her a furious glance. 'I wasn't just

using you! There was nothing fake about my desire for you… However, if I'd known in advance that you were *that* innocent, I like to think I would have stepped back. Unfortunately, you didn't give me that choice.'

'Sev…you didn't give me one single choice about *any* of this!' Amy pointed out in strong rebuttal. 'And naturally I believed that your interest in me was genuine.'

'It *is* genuine!' Sev slammed back at her, losing patience with her accusations. 'We wouldn't even be having this conversation if it wasn't. If your only value to me was the fact that you're Oliver Lawson's daughter, you wouldn't even be here now. We would be finished.'

A humourless laugh fell from Amy's dry lips. 'We're finished anyway. You dressed me up like a doll tonight and took me out to humiliate and hurt me.'

'I did not,' Sev sliced in stark denial.

'Oh, yes, you did. You introduced me in a public place to a father who looked at me in disgust, a father I can only be ashamed of,' she extended tightly, struggling to contain her turbulent emotions. 'That was information I should have received in private. I deserved better than that kind of treatment, Sev. And what about Oliver's wife, Cecily?'

'What about her?' Sev queried with a bemused frown.

'You humiliated her as well and, like me, she was an innocent party. Couldn't you have had some consideration and taken your revenge in a way that was less painful for me and for her? No,' Amy answered curtly for herself. 'You wouldn't have done that because you wanted to be in at the kill and see my father's face as you exposed him. But that doesn't excuse you any more than your sister's hurt excuses you for harming innocent people.'

'I have not harmed you in any way!' Sev shot back at her with a growling edge of frustration.

'Do I *look* happy to you? Did it ever occur to you that I may have had a dream about my unknown father, a dream in which I had *one* parent who, if he actually met me, wouldn't despise me? And did it ever occur to you while you were playing your vengeful games that I could be falling in love with you? In love with a guy who doesn't actually exist in the real world? A guy you were only *pretending* to be?' Amy fired back at him shakily, her voice rising in tune with her distress.

'You've only known me for a couple of weeks,' Sev parried in scorching dismissal. 'Nobody falls in love that fast or that easily.'

And he was so confident that he was right in that assumption, she recognised painfully as the colour in her clammy face drained away. But *she* had fallen for him like a ton of bricks, possibly because she hadn't loved before, possibly because she had never met a man so attractive before, and she had trusted him instinctively and had let down all her defences. Now she felt gutted and guilty that she had been so susceptible, so *weak*.

'I think I hate you and that should tell you a lot about how I feel,' Amy said tightly. 'I've never hated anyone before. I believe it's time I went home.'

'I want you to stay. I want to talk this out,' Sev fired back at her impatiently.

'There can be no talking it out. What's done is done…and you're not even sorry, which says it all really,' Amy muttered in a brittle undertone. 'You don't understand or accept that what you did to me tonight was cruel and wrong…and that this whole pretence you went through with me was even more dishonest and shameful. Everything was a lie.'

'No, it wasn't!' Sev bit out rawly, his fists clenching. 'I only concealed what I knew about you when we first met. That was the *sole* pretence! Everything since then has been one hundred per cent truthful and real.'

'Sev, you only brought me into your life and kept me there to ensure that I went to that party tonight…how is that not a pretence? How is that real?'

The silence stretched taut as a rubber band stretched too tight.

'Do I still qualify for a lift home?' Amy enquired abruptly, standing at the front door, thinking that *nothing* about Sev had been real. He hadn't really been a nice guy, blind to the difference in their social status and income. In truth, whatever she had looked like and however she had behaved, Sev had intended to march her out to confront her father with his daughter at that party.

'*Dio mio...*' Sev bit out. 'What the hell do you think I am?'

'A devious bastard with about as much decent feeling, compassion and humility as the average rock,' Amy framed unevenly. 'Tell me one last thing—are you planning to keep Harley or was that also a confidence trick designed to impress me?'

'Of course I'm keeping Harley!' Sev thundered back at her.

'Do you know why you prefer animals to people?' Amy breathed fiercely. 'Animals don't care about your morals and they don't answer back.'

'Is that it? Are you finished now?' Sev shot

at her in the rushing silence that seemed to assault her ears. Her stomach was churning, and her chest was tight. Even sucking in a breath hurt. It had just dawned on her that she was never ever going to see him again and that felt like a hammer blow even though she knew it shouldn't, even though she knew she had had a lucky escape, a welcome wake-up call to reality, whatever anyone wanted to call it.

'Yes, I'm finished,' she murmured flatly, and it was true, she had nothing left to say. He had hurt her and there was nothing she could do about it. She wasn't connected to Sev, she wasn't close to him, she wasn't anything she had thought she was. Talking to a guy like him about love was a joke, a pathetic, foolish joke, and she wished she had kept her mouth shut.

'Reconsider,' Sev urged in a grudging, deep undertone as he drew out his phone. 'I won't run after you…that's not my style.'

'I'll live,' Amy told him, unable to resist the urge to steal a last look at him, violet eyes scanning the sheer chiselled beauty of his proud dark features. Her gaze lingered on the artful hollows and angles of his spectacular bone structure that lent him such charismatic presence, and took in the challenge of those liquid-bronze eyes that telegraphed more angry frustration than remorse. She lifted her chin in defiance and turned away again.

Within minutes she was tucked into the limousine, travelling home in style for the last time ever, and painful tears were squeezing out below her lowered eyelids, stinging her skin as they trickled down her cheeks, slow and silent in their fall. She sucked in a steadying breath and forced herself to look out of the window at the brightly lit shops. Christmas would be here soon, and she wasn't about to let him spoil Christmas as well, was she?

She would allow herself one night to grieve, she told herself ruefully. Sev had just been a dream that didn't pan out, a silly girlish fantasy. She should have smelt a rat from the outset when a guy of his calibre showed interest in someone as ordinary as she was, but who didn't want to believe that a dream could come true? She had been too busy being flattered, charmed and seduced by his interest and she had stopped using her brain, hadn't even looked for flaws and inconsistencies. At least Harley had got a home out of it all! She pressed her trembling hands to her face and told herself to stop beating herself up for what she couldn't help or change. She would survive, she had survived worse, she told herself dully.

Ironically and for the first time ever she was feeling sympathy for her late mother. What must it have been like for Lorraine to watch the man she loved pursue the boss's daughter? And then for him to come back to her after the wedding, doubtless raising her hopes of reconciliation again? Amy grimaced. Somewhere deep down inside where she didn't explore very often she had had a little dream that her mother might have been wrong about her father and that he might, after all, have wanted her more than he had been prepared to admit. But she had seen the ugly truth of that childish dream in Oliver Lawson's stricken face that very evening. He had been horrified by her appearance and clearly much more concerned about how his unfortunate wife would react to the revelation of Amy's existence and how that might impact on his own life. And poor, unhappy Annabel, Amy thought sadly, who had pinned her romantic hopes on such a lying, cheating coward of a man, who didn't know what fidelity, or the truth, was.

Amy curled up in her bed with Hopper. She had never felt as alone in her life as she did at that moment. The evening, the fantasy outing in the gorgeous dress, had started out with such promise and she had been so excited, *so* happy, and then it had all come crashing down like a roof on top of her and had almost buried her alive. Had Sev been right? Was it impossible to fall in love so fast? She hoped he was right. She didn't want to feel gutted and miserable for months on end. Maybe it was only an infatuation, a sort of adult crush that would fade as swiftly as it had begun, especially now that he was out of her life again. At least she hadn't told him that she loved him. She had only hung that possibility, that risk out there and he had looked at her in disbelief, as if she were certifiably insane.

He would give her a week to cool off, Sev decided grimly as he savoured his whiskey before heading for bed...*alone*! Not what he had expected, not what he had wanted. No woman had ever walked out on him before, especially not after he had admitted a particular interest. He had never done that before either, he acknowledged, didn't know what it was about Amy, he only knew that when she had walked out of that door with her nose in the air he had wanted to physically yank her back and *make* her see sense. No one in their right mind would turn their back on the kind of chemistry they shared, he assured himself bracingly.

Amy had been hurt and understandably

angry. Lawson had hurt her just as he had hurt Annabel, staring with cold distaste at her as though she had climbed up out of the gutter to confront him. Bastard! But if Sev had told Amy in advance of his plans, she would never have agreed to take part because she was far too kind to people in general… although not to him, he conceded angrily, his strong jawline clenching as he tried to recall when, if ever, his moral standards had been questioned. She had held *him* to account though, like a hanging judge and executioner.

Not quite the pushover he had assumed, he conceded, still furious with her and unable to sleep for the first time in years. She had made him feel guilty for setting her up, for putting her in that position with her sperm donor, but it wasn't as though he could go back and change anything he had done now. A shame he refused to acknowledge or consider sat like a giant stone on his chest because Amy had been correct on one score: he hadn't considered her feelings or Cecily Lawson's when he'd plotted his revenge.

Lawson would also be hearing from Sev's lawyer concerning future arrangements for child support for Annabel's child. That would end the whole horrid business and draw a line under it…though not if Sev lost Amy over his night's work, he conceded ruefully.

He could tell her that he was sorry, even if that was untrue. He was sorry he had hurt her, sorry he had lacked the foresight to see what that scene with her father would do to a woman as tender-hearted as Amy was. But he still *wasn't* sorry for hitting back hard at Lawson for his misdoings. The instant that lowering idea of apologising crept into his brain, Sev turned over and punched his pillow in frustration. It would be a cold day in hell before he gave her a second chance! There were plenty of women out there in the world and few of them would question his principles. And they would also know better than to mention love. *Love!* Sev winced. Maybe he had dodged a bullet there; maybe she would have turned clingy.

Why was it that that idea wasn't the turn-off it usually was? Why was it that the concept of Amy being clingy had the opposite effect? If she started phoning or texting him all the time, well, at least what she had to say was interesting and she was very undemanding and easy to be with, as well as absolutely everything he had ever dreamt of in bed. In the strangest way, she matched him…or at least, she *had…*

He could cope with clingy, he decided, as long as she got the love stuff out of her head and grew up a little. *Sì*, he could cope with clingy fine. Nobody was perfect, after all. She would text him, he surmised. She would save face by asking him about Harley or even Annabel, he thought confidently. He would have her back long before Christmas.

CHAPTER EIGHT

AMY EMERGED FROM seeing her doctor even paler than when she had arrived at the surgery.

Although she had believed it was impossible, although she had thought she was safe from the risk, she was pregnant with Sev's baby. Over the past ten days she had been sick on two occasions, had developed a strange sensitivity towards the smell of frying food and her breasts had moved up half a cup size while also becoming painfully tender. She had taken a pregnancy test when her period was late just to reassure herself that there was nothing to worry about, only to learn that there was very definitely something to worry about.

It had been ten days since the party. As December advanced, all around her the Christmas season was gathering steam. Customers at the café were chatting about office parties and arriving laden with shopping and their children were bursting with anticipation. She hadn't seen Sev again but unbelievably he had sent her flowers. Flowers with a card.

Waiting to hear from you

And ironically that had actually made her laugh, because it was textbook Sev to be bold and not to give an inch and there wasn't much that roused her amusement in her current existence, which was just work, work and more work and now worry into the bargain. It was demoralising to appreciate that she had repeated her mother's mistake and conceived by a man who would want neither her nor her child. A man who had casually sent her the most gorgeous bouquet just as if he hadn't broken her stupid heart. Well, wouldn't a pregnancy be a shock for him? she thought unhappily. Not to mention a huge shock for her, but she honestly hadn't thought it was possible.

Only the test she had carried out for herself had told her that it *was* possible. The doctor in the clinic had reminded her that when she had recently changed to a different brand of pill she had been warned to take extra precautions for a month. She didn't remember being told that, but perhaps her mind had been wandering because at the time, without an active sex life, the threat of consequences had not been something to worry about. Then there had been the bug she had succumbed to that same week, which would also have weakened her protection. Of course, none of that would have mattered had *Sev* remembered to use a condom. She reminded herself of that oversight on his part. They had both been very careless.

She texted him on the way home, a clutch of leaflets in her hand and a date organised for her first scan.

Need to see you urgently.

My house tonight. I'll pick you up at six-thirty.

No, somewhere more neutral…but private.

A bar?

Amy deliberated and then agreed. At least if they were somewhere public they were less likely to have a row and she could get up and leave any time that she wanted. She returned to the shelter, which was abnormally quiet. Harold had surprised her by closing the surgery for two days, explaining that he had important appointments to keep. He had been unusually evasive with her as well when she'd asked questions and it was a surprise to her to climb the stairs to her room and find her boss and a stranger standing chatting outside her door.

Harold looked awkward. 'Amy…this is my son, George. I've been showing George round our little domain. Would you be willing to let him see your room, just to see the size of it?'

'Of course.' Amy was only slightly surprised that she had not had the chance to meet George before, because he had been working abroad as a veterinary surgeon for several years.

The younger man nodded. 'That would be helpful…if you don't mind?'

'Not a problem.' Amy undid the lock that had been installed on the door when she moved in the year before. She was wondering what the size of her room had to do with anything. They glanced in and talked in low voices and, eventually, Harold gave her a smile of thanks and went back downstairs. Amy was tired, ridiculously tired, she thought, considering that she had had the day off, and she lay down on the bed to take a short nap, wanting to be firing on all possible cylinders by the time she met up with Sev.

When she told him her news, he would be shocked and angry, she thought heavily, probably reacting much as her father had twenty-odd years earlier because an unplanned pregnancy between two people who were not a couple was clearly a problem. But what could she do about that? And she was only telling him as a courtesy, not seeking his advice or support or anything else. Would he be disappointed that she wasn't even prepared to consider a termination? Well, what did it matter if he was?

Amy didn't have a single living relative aside of the father who didn't want any contact with her, and she wanted her child, regardless of how difficult raising her baby alone would be. When her baby was born, she would have a family for the first time ever and she savoured that concept. Yes, it would be tough going it alone as a parent, but other women managed and why shouldn't she, when she was willing to work hard? She was relieved that she would, at least, have completed her apprenticeship by the time her child was born, because that would equip her for a decent job in the future.

All those sensible thoughts aside, Amy's drowsy brain centred back on Sev, lingering on unforgotten moments with Sev's lean, hard body arching over hers and giving her the most incredible pleasure. Guiltily shelving that recollection, she curled up tighter.

* * *

While Amy dozed that afternoon, Sev struggled to concentrate on work. He had assumed that Amy would cave sooner. Ten days was longer than he had expected to wait to hear from her again and he had been mulling over other possible approaches before she texted him while at the same time reminding himself that he intended to allow her to walk away and stay away, that she was scarcely irreplaceable, that he had many other tempting options. Only that inner pep talk hadn't worked because his libido seemed to have centred on her, so that the allure of other women, and the appeal of the variety he had always thought so necessary to his comfort, had faded. Was that because Amy had now made herself a challenge?

Was he one of those strange men doomed to only really *want* a woman who seemed unavailable? A bored man in need of novelty, who could only seriously desire what he couldn't have? The suspicion bothered him, not least because he kept on breaking his own strict rules with Amy. He had had sex with her even though he had promised himself at the outset that he would not do so. He had taken her home, kept her there *all night* and his hunger for her had still not been sated. But it would get messy with Amy, drama queen that she was, he reflected grimly.

Did it ever occur to you...that I could be falling in love with you?

Who the hell said that to a guy she had only spent one night with? True, it had been an extraordinary night, but they had still only shared one night and a handful of meetings. And what was with the *'urgently'* in that text of hers? In their relationship nothing could be urgent...

Except his desire to have her again, he acknowledged, a desire that kept him hard and aching. So, was he planning to forgive her? She had infuriated him, offended him. He leant back in his office chair and cursed. His mind, his thoughts were all over the place, not concentrated as was the norm for him. A lean brown fist clenched. He wanted his peace of mind back, his ability to focus. Was she the key?

He was willing to admit that he had screwed up with Amy. The sex had muddied the waters. He should have resisted her, *not* slept with her, at least not until that party was over and the truth was out. He could do nothing now to change anything that had happened, although it should have occurred to him sooner that Amy would be hurt by her father's indifference and that she would blame him for that experience.

As for her accusation that he had neither compassion nor decency, that was categorically untrue. A lack of humility? Well, he was willing to own up to that flaw. He had tasted enough humility as a persecuted child to ensure that he would rarely be humble without good cause as an adult. In addition, he possessed the fierce confidence of a guy who very rarely found himself in the wrong.

But whether he liked it or not, he *had* gone wrong with Amy. But if he could go back, would he be willing to forgo the pleasure of seeing Lawson's face freeze and pale when he realised who Amy was? No, he had gained too much satisfaction from that moment to regret it, particularly when he thought of his sister's tears and the hollow look of hurt that still haunted her eyes. Annabel had been bright and bubbly and happy until Lawson got hold of her and crushed her spirit and her ability to trust.

But that said, Sev was even angrier that Amy had been hurt too and that he had to accept that he had recklessly, *blindly* caused that hurt. As for Lawson's wife, well, he hadn't thought of her at all, except as a sort of *deus ex machina*, who would hopefully punish Lawson even more for him. He felt vaguely sorry for the woman, but she had to have some idea of the nature of the man to whom she had been married for over twenty years.

Getting ready to meet Sev at the upmarket bar in Highgate, Amy would not allow herself to make a special effort. She wouldn't

be staying long; she wouldn't be trying to attract him. There was no longer anything between them, although the birth of their child
would change that, she thought in shock acceptance of the link that would be created
between them. If Sev planned to be involved
with their child, she would have to work on
having a more friendly relationship with him.
She shrugged, reckoning that the occasional
smile and polite word would suffice if their
paths crossed. That would cost her little but,
for all she knew, he wouldn't be interested in
access to their son or daughter. He might not
be too much different from her own father.

Petting Hopper and tucking him back in
his cage with the promise of a future treat,
she headed for the Tube station. The meeting place was a fashionable bar and busy. She
picked her way through the throng, feeling
underdressed in her somewhat shabby black
sweater and jeans amidst all the smartly
dressed office workers congregated round
the bar, her anxious gaze engaged in skim-
ming round the room in search of Sev. He

lifted a lean brown hand to signal her from a corner booth, which would mercifully offer them, she realised, a fair amount of privacy.

It was now or never, Sev registered grimly. He had to apologise, *had* to bite the bullet and hope that that climbdown worked some magic for him. He wanted his life back to normal and it didn't feel normal any more without Amy. He didn't understand that extraordinary fact, but didn't need to understand it to know that he wanted her back, wanted to see her smile at him again. And if the miracle cure to the emptiness dogging him was an apology, he was determined to give it a go, even if on some level the concept still struck him as humiliating.

Sev signalling her, Amy thought painfully, suddenly reminded her painfully of their first encounter at the café, and she stilled before she remembered that that had all been one big fake from his supposed interest to his every question. Now pale and taut, she sank down on the bench opposite him and fought not to be electrified with excitement by his eyes glinting at her from below the lush black screen of his lashes.

'Hi,' she muttered awkwardly, her fingers plucking nervously at the cuffs of her sweater.

Sev breathed in deep, afraid of losing his momentum. 'I'm sorry I hurt you,' he murmured quietly, apologising for the first time ever to a woman. 'That was never my intention. I'm afraid I didn't spend any time thinking about how that little confrontation would impact on you.'

'We don't need to talk about that any more,' Amy told him uncomfortably, her facial muscles tightening for she saw no point now in going back over still-sensitive subjects, but she was relieved that he had ultimately recognised his mistakes. 'I think we did the topic to death and it's behind us now.'

'What would you like to drink?' Sev asked as a waitress appeared by the edge of the table and stared at Sev as though he had walked off a movie screen in front of her.

'Just a water for me, please.' With his attention momentarily distracted, Amy feasted her attention on him, noting the shadow of dark stubble accentuating his sculpted jaw line and beautifully full sensual mouth, and suppressing a shiver to stare down at the leopard-print table surface instead. Remembering his mouth on her body, she felt hot all over and she pressed her thighs together, fighting to shut out those embarrassingly intimate memories, which now felt inappropriate. But it was a challenge because Sev *did* look exactly as though he had walked off a movie screen. His sheer masculine beauty made him incredibly noticeable.

Sev studied her with an odd little smile that lit his stunning eyes to gleaming gold and quirked his mobile mouth. 'So…what is *so* urgent?' he prompted in a distinctly playful tone.

Amy breathed in deep as her bottle of water arrived and then swallowed hard as she poured it into a glass. 'It's something serious.'

'Lawson hasn't been in touch with you, has

he?' Sev demanded in a concerned undertone. 'I assumed he hadn't kept tabs on you and wouldn't know where you lived but *if*—'

'No...er...it's nothing to do with him,' Amy hastened to assure him.

Soft colour had lit up her cheeks and as she stared down at her glass, the very image of awkwardness, Sev wanted to reach across the table and haul her into his arms, an urge that shook him when he was trying to play it cool. Although, he reasoned, playing it cool with Amy, who hadn't a clue about how to play anything cool, was kind of surplus to requirements and might indeed lead to them sitting there saying nothing of importance all evening if he left the control of events in her hands.

Looking at her, though, was a treat, he acknowledged, stretching out his long legs in the vague hope of easing the taut fit of his trousers across the groin. She was wearing a sweater so large and long and loose, it might have been said that the sweater was wearing her, but the black against her hair accentuated the sunshine gold of its colour and the pink in her cheeks enhanced those violet eyes, making them seem more purple than ever. He could see faint dark shadows beneath, though, that hinted at sleepless nights, and he liked that suspicion, indeed *hoped* she had tossed and turned a few nights the way he had.

'I'm pregnant, Sev,' she whispered baldly.

And it was as if the world stopped turning for Sev, spinning him off unprepared into foreign territory, and he lost colour and froze.

'And it *has* to be yours,' she added to prevent him from asking that question in the awful sudden silence, which sat like a brick wall between them and the loud bar chatter. 'You're probably wondering how.'

At that, Sev flung his dark head back, liquid-bronze eyes narrowed, steady. 'No, I'm not wondering. I was irresponsible. What do you want to do?'

That simple question plunged right to the heart of the matter and his impressive calm reassured her that an ugly scene or recriminations were unlikely. 'I want to have the baby,' she almost whispered, bracing herself for a critical comment.

Sev released his breath in a slow measured hiss. 'OK.'

'That's what was urgent,' Amy explained. 'But I don't want anything from you. I can tell you that now. Letting you know about this is just a courtesy.'

Sev's bronze gaze blazed brilliant gold. 'Just a courtesy,' he repeated, his dark deep drawl almost swallowing the phrase.

How the hell was it just a courtesy to tell him when it was *his* child as well? But he said nothing, reluctant to say anything that might upset or alienate her. Why? At that moment, she might as well have had a little heavenly halo blossoming over her head etched with the immortal words, *mother of my unborn child*. And he *knew* he had to be cautious with what he said and what he did. Even so, he wasn't planning to sit back and hope for the best as his own rather naïve father had done when his pregnant fiancée had changed her mind about marrying him. Nor was he prepared to watch from a distance as she inevitably brought other father figures into her life to bring up his child.

'I would like to be involved,' Sev murmured quietly. '*Fully* involved...'

Amy nodded, wondering why she had the strangest suspicion that she was sitting dangerously close to a ticking time bomb as goose flesh broke out on her skin below her sweater. 'What would that entail?'

'I would like to come to scans and stuff.'

'No. I wouldn't like that.' Amy rebutted the idea of that instantly.

'Perhaps you could share them after you receive them,' Sev said stiffly, shifting gear at that first tacit refusal but maintaining his assurance. 'I would also like to help you financially now or in any other way that would be helpful to you.'

'No...er...no,' Amy interrupted in dismay. 'Nothing like that will be necessary until the baby is born. I can manage fine until then.

I've got a job and somewhere to live. I'm all right for now.'

In consternation, Sev watched her push away her glass and stand up. 'Where are you going?'

'Home,' she told him apologetically. 'I mean... I've said all I need to say and so have you. Everything's up in the air right now, so we don't need to discuss anything else.'

'Up in the air?' he queried with a frown.

'Well, look at what almost happened to your sister,' Amy reminded him reluctantly. 'Sometimes, things can go wrong.'

'Nothing's going to go wrong,' Sev broke in confidently and he closed a hand over hers to hold her back as she began to turn away. 'And I'm here, always available to help you at any time. You have my number. Anything you need in the future, you can depend on me.'

Tears of surprise and relief burned at the backs of her strained eyes. 'I tend to try not to depend on other people, Sev,' she warned him.

'I'm not other people. I'm the father of your baby,' Sev contradicted. 'You can't go through this alone.'

Amy replayed that conversation in her head and the feel of that warm hand on hers all the way home on the train. There was a note on her door from Harold, asking her to come in fifteen minutes before the start of the morning surgery. Wondering if her boss was planning to come clean and tell her why he had shut the surgery down for a couple of days, she set her alarm and went to bed early, still thinking about Sev. He had been really decent, she conceded grudgingly. He hadn't got angry or stressed, nor had he tried to impose his views on her. He had been calm and accepting. In truth she could not have hoped for a more positive response.

As she walked into Harold's tiny office the following morning, she noticed that the older man looked grey and weary, the lines on his face more heavily etched than they had been several weeks earlier.

'Come in and sit down, Amy. I'm sure

you've been wondering what's happening here this week and I'm about to explain. My son will be taking over the practice from next Monday,' he advised her.

Amy blinked rapidly. 'Your son,' she echoed uncertainly.

'And I'm afraid that for that to happen an awful lot of things will be changing,' Harold told her heavily. 'I've got cancer. The prognosis for recovery is good but I'm facing a long course of treatment and I can't put off my retirement any longer.'

'I'm so sorry,' Amy murmured in shock, trying not to selfishly wonder what the coming changeover would mean to her on a personal basis. 'I understand your position.'

'Firstly, I'm afraid the charity will have to be closed down. This place will no longer be a functioning animal shelter. George isn't interested in taking that on and he intends to expand into that space and use it for other things.' Scanning her shattered face, the older man sighed. 'The shelter was always Cordy's project and I only continued it after her death because I felt that that was my duty. However, that's no longer possible and our current residents will have to be farmed out to other rescue organisations.'

Amy was so devastated by that announcement that she could barely catch her breath and she simply nodded. Harold knew as well as she did that his decision meant that some of their animals might end up being euthanised. Her throat closed over at the image of Hopper, alone in a cage, awaiting termination. She felt sick.

'And now we come to the more personal aspects of these major changes,' her boss continued reluctantly. 'George has big plans to remodel here and you will no longer be able to use the storage room as accommodation. He's willing to give you a month's notice to find somewhere else but, to be frank, I had to argue for that because George doesn't think I should ever have agreed to let you live on the premises in the first place.'

Amy nodded jerkily, her mouth too dry to form words. 'And my apprenticeship?'

Harold Bunting frowned, fulfilling her worst fears. 'George already has a full staff and, as he works in a highly specialised field of surgery, you wouldn't qualify for his team,' he admitted apologetically. 'I have emailed all my contacts to see if I can find another placement for you, because you do only have another few months to do to complete your course. All I can say in finishing, Amy, is that I'm very sorry that these changes will disrupt your life as well. Right now, you have time off. The surgery won't be reopening until George takes over here.'

Amy tottered up out of her seat, knowing that there was nothing she could say or do to change anything. She expressed her best wishes for the older man's recovery and promised to start looking for other accommodation immediately. She waited until the nausea receded and then put Hopper on a leash and went out for a walk, praying that the cool air would clear her pounding head.

What on earth was she going to do next? Pregnant, homeless and now out of work as well? The sheer immensity of the blows that had come her way without warning consumed her and, beyond that, fear of what would happen to the shelter animals hung over her like a dark threatening cloud. But she didn't blame Harold for what was happening, not in the slightest. The rescue shelter had always been Cordy's particular love, rather than her partner's, and poor Harold had quite enough to be dealing with right now with his illness. She had kept her composure for *his* sake, knowing he didn't need to be faced with a tearful, self-pitying meltdown.

She was in over her head, she acknowledged shakily as she sat in a small park, Hopper stationed at her knee. Twenty-three dogs and six cats and two rabbits needed a home. She needed a home, a job, an income to live on. Her head felt as if it would burst with the number of anxieties that were eating her alive. And she pulled out her phone and breathed in deep and slow. When it came to the needs of the animals she had been looking after and loving for so long, pride didn't deserve a look-in.

She texted Sev, laid it all out for him—the charity to be closed, the animals to be moved out, her loss of employment and home.

I need your help.

She gritted her teeth as she added the words, because approaching him warred with every proud, independent skin cell she had, and she had to stiffen her backbone to hit 'send'.

CHAPTER NINE

SEV READ THE text in the middle of a board meeting and his shrewd brain homed straight to the essentials: twenty-three dogs, six cats, two bunnies and Amy to house. Fate was giving him a second chance, he grasped, a chance to redeem himself.

Why? Amy *hated* him and he could not afford to ignore that and hope she got over it if he wanted a future relationship with his child. In the bar, she had shrunk away from him when he'd grabbed her hand to stop her leaving. She had avoided eye contact, indeed had evaded any hint of the personal in their conversation. Her lack of understanding and forgiveness, her failure to warm up on meeting him had come as a shock to Sev, who had assumed that the essential caring softness of her nature meant that she would be more pliable, more easily brought round to his way of thinking. Only she hadn't even given him the chance to change her outlook and then she had stopped him dead and silenced him with her announcement.

He was excited about the baby and that had shaken him even more. He didn't even care how it had happened. He knew it was the deserved result of a man who had forgotten birth control *once* by accident and then had deliberately *repeated* the oversight for the remainder of the night because he had enjoyed it so much. In other words, whatever flaw her contraception had developed was as nothing when set next to his own sheer recklessness. Beyond that, Sev was struggling to deal with the problem of what might well prove to be one of the most important relationships in his life, with Amy, when he had already wrecked it.

The mother of his child didn't trust him, and he had only himself to blame for that state of affairs. Even worse, he had hurt her and now she was on her guard. Sev didn't want to be treated like the enemy, he wanted to *share* the experience, but Amy was already putting up barriers. He knew how much pain his own father had suffered at being excluded from his son's life and the guilt he still felt at his failure to gain access to Sev as a little boy. Regrettably his father had not been wealthy enough to field a legal team capable of taking on the top-flight Aiken lawyers. Lack of money, however, was the least of Sev's problems.

For a very rich man, Sev did not own many homes. In fact, there were only three: two in the UK and one in Italy, and two of those three inherited from relatives. He used hotels when he travelled. But he had one country property in the UK, he reminded himself, the much-fought-over Oaktree Hall in Surrey, the birthplace of his maternal grandfather, gifted to him at twenty-one along with his substantial trust fund. His mother had been enraged because she had long wanted that property for herself, for its snobby ancestral connections and proximity to London, not to mention the homes of several minor royals. He had rented the property out for years, but it was currently empty, a great barn of a place with a vast cluster of outbuildings from its days as a working country estate. There would surely be room there for twenty-three dogs, six cats, two bunnies and one petite pregnant woman?

Cancelling the meeting, Sev put the problem of the charity to be dissolved into the hands of one of his finance team and began to make plans. He was worried about Amy. The last thing she needed in her current condition was stress. He devoted the rest of his day to exploring Oaktree Hall as a viable option, checking the condition of the place and putting his PA onto the task of hiring local staff and equipping the house for occupation. Those demands met, he visited the veterinary surgery in the village nearby to get the answers to certain questions and nothing that he learned there was likely to please Amy, he conceded ruefully. On the other hand, if his plans were agreeable to her, she would have a huge amount of other stuff to keep her busy. He worried that it would all be too much for her and that, rather than releasing her from stress, he would actually be giving her more.

Sev rang Amy late that evening. 'I may have found somewhere for you and the animals…a new base,' he told her briefly. 'But you'll need to see it to tell me what you think before I make any further arrangements.'

'Me *and* the animals?' she emphasised in astonishment.

'Yes, but you'd be in charge of them and their needs. I can get you help but it would be a huge responsibility for you to take on,' he warned her worriedly.

'Oh, I could do it…yes, I definitely could!' she rushed to assure him.

Sev felt momentarily guilty for having baited the trap and set it to ensnare her but he wanted her back, he wanted her safe and happy, and it was just a fact of life that making Amy happy meant throwing a lot of animals into the mix. 'I'll pick you up tomorrow at ten,' he told her.

'Even if this doesn't work out, thanks for trying,' Amy said gratefully.

'I see no reason why it shouldn't work out,' Sev told her confidently.

He dined with Annabel that evening. When she enquired about Amy, he admitted that he had messed up with her. She asked him what he had done and frowned when he refused to give her details. He told her about Amy's current predicament and explained what he was hoping to do. By the time he had finished speaking, his sister was staring at him in growing wonderment.

'Sev to the rescue? Since when were you a white knight for anyone but me?'

'Amy's pregnant and the baby is mine,' Sev volunteered between clenched teeth, because baring his soul did not come naturally to him, but he had to be honest with Annabel because sooner or later she would discover that Amy was Oliver Lawson's daughter and she would make her own deductions about what had gone wrong between them. Annabel had told him that she had heard from Oliver's solicitor with regard to future financial support for the baby she was carrying but she had heard nothing more from her child's father, which seemed to be a source of relief to her after the upsetting arguments that had previously taken place between them.

Annabel gave him a shocked appraisal, concern softening her eyes. 'Oh, poor Amy… and all that happening right on top of a new pregnancy…how ghastly.'

'Not to mention me having let her down before she found out that she had conceived,' Sev dropped in grittily. 'I have a lot of ground to make up.'

Amy didn't sleep much that night and wakened early, glancing round the small room that had become her home and feeling sad that she had to leave it. For years though her life had been subject to sudden moves and changes. There had been the move into a council-run children's home from her mother's apartment, followed by her passage through several foster homes before she had made the wonderful move to Cordy's cosy house. Ultimately that stability had been wrenched from her again and she had ended up in the surgery's store room, simply grateful for the free roof over her head.

Amy was masking a yawn with an embarrassed hand as she climbed into Sev's limo. He was working on a laptop and when he immediately flipped it shut, she flushed uncomfortably and said hurriedly, 'Oh, don't stop working on my account... I'm half asleep anyway.'

Even so, her drowsy eyes clung to him while he worked, lingering on the dark downbent head with the wonderfully glossy black hair that she remembered running her fingers through *that* night, the chiselled perfection of his strong profile. Colour heightening as a wave of guilty heat engulfed her, Amy dredged her attention off him again and sat face forward instead, but the image of him lingered, sleek and sophisticated even in tailored chinos and a casual jacket teamed with an open-necked green shirt. Fabric sheathed his long powerful thighs, shaping lean hips and a narrow waist as effectively as fine wool defined his broad shoulders. And beneath the clothes, he looked even better, she found herself thinking, recalling the lean, taut golden musculature of his chest and taut stomach and quivering inside her skin. At that point she wanted to slap herself to somehow suppress the steady march of mortifyingly sexual reactions he awakened in her. It was like a hunger that never quite quit, a hunger she hadn't known until she met him, and it embarrassed her to death.

'Why do you have to move from above the surgery at such short notice?' Sev enquired abruptly, endeavouring not to stare at her soft full pink lips and imagine what she could do with them, but evidently his body hadn't got that message. Even when she was casually garbed in the same shapeless black sweater and jeans, there was something spookily sensual and appealing about Amy and she didn't need to bare an inch of flesh to exercise that power over him.

'I don't have the right to expect much notice,' Amy explained. 'It was an unofficial arrangement that I could use a storage room to live in until I finished my course.'

'A *storage* room?' Sev cut in, his astonishment palpable. 'You're living in a storage room? I thought you were using a caretaker's flat on that floor.'

'No, there's only storage upstairs. My boss was doing me a *real* favour,' Amy informed him. 'I don't earn enough to pay a decent rent. I've been comfortable enough staying there. I have a mini oven in my room and use the surgery washroom downstairs.'

'Paying you a living wage would have been the better option,' Sev commented drily, believing that her employer had been taking advantage by keeping her conveniently on site, while being equally aware that she would not accept that view.

'My boss is already paying for a full-time nurse. I'm not able to do much more than grunt work until I qualify,' Amy retorted wryly. 'Everything was easier when Cordy was alive because I wasn't paying rent to live with her, but after she passed, I had to move out and London rents are extortionate. There was nothing within my budget.'

'And yet you told me that you didn't *need* my financial help?' Sev censured.

'I was managing fine until all this happened. Everything going wrong at once hasn't left me any choices or much time, and the chances of Harold finding me a placement with another vet at this time of year are slim to none, never mind where I would find to rent with my budget.' She sighed. 'Where are we going?'

'Somewhere in the country that has space for the rescue animals as well.'

Amy sat bolt upright in the seat beside him, her triangular face lighting up with sudden intense interest, and he almost laughed, not at all surprised that she was more concerned about the animals than herself. '*Seriously? All* of them? Where? How?'

'It's a country house with outbuildings. My English great-grandfather built it in the nineteen-twenties, and I inherited it as my mother's eldest son. I've never used it, so it was rented out for years.'

'Why haven't you used it?'

'It's too big for a single man. Most recently it was used as the backdrop for a costume-drama series on television. I can't sell the place because it's tied up in a trust and if I have a son or a daughter, it will eventually go to him or her.'

Her smooth brow furrowed in surprise. 'But *that* means…'

'Yes. *My* firstborn inherits it, a state of affairs that enraged my mother. She tried to fight the trust because she wanted her second son to inherit rather than me,' he murmured wryly. 'But sadly for her, my great-grandfather was also illegitimate and he didn't want any of his descendants to be disinherited for that reason, and the terms of the trust are quite clear on that score.'

'Why do you have such a bad relationship with your mother?' Amy asked curiously.

'I think it's because I'm her only regret, the

one blemish in her perfect world. I'll always be the reminder that she met my father before my stepfather and that her younger son, Devon, may inherit my stepfather's baronetcy, but the trust ensured that I received the bulk of her family's money and the original ancestral home. That made me the source of envy and resentment in the Aiken family, but it also gave me my independence from them and allowed me to set up my own business at a young age,' Sev pointed out quietly. 'I've learned to accept the rough with the smooth.'

'What's your father's family like?'

Sev laughed. 'Refreshingly normal. I have four half-brothers, only one of whom is married, and my stepmother treats me like an honorary son. I don't see as much of them as I should, but I've invited them to join me for Christmas this year. I'd be grateful if you were willing to help out with that.'

'Help out…how?' Amy exclaimed in surprise just as the limousine drove down a lane to stop outside a paved courtyard surrounded by buildings.

'We'll talk about that later. Now, I'll show you the stables first, see what you think,' Sev murmured, his long legs carrying him in the direction of a stone archway, leaving her almost running to keep up.

He showed her round a stable yard in good repair, walked her through a series of outhouses and finally into a large empty barn. The occasional light guiding touch of a hand at her spine made her quiver like a jelly inside herself just as the dark deep rasp of his masculine voice close to her ear made everything in her body tighten.

'It's not perfect, but if you agree I can have sectional cages erected in the barn within forty-eight hours,' Sev proffered.

Amy blinked rapidly and stared up at him, astonished by the amount of thought and planning he had already clearly put into settling her problems for her. '*Proper* kennels? Sev…don't go to so much trouble and expense, because there's ample room here for the animals, but isn't the yard used for anything else?'

'No. The land's rented out now and these buildings are redundant unless I start keeping horses here again, which I might do if I was living here on a more regular basis,' he mused thoughtfully.

'Why would you do all this for me?' she whispered.

Sev sent her a winging sardonic glance from narrowed eyes that gleamed like precious gold in the winter sunshine. The lush black lashes surrounding his gaze only heightened their sensual appeal and she averted her scrutiny in haste as the zinging energy of her response made her core clench.

'We both know why,' he parried. 'I screwed up with you and I'm trying to make up for it.'

Amazed by that blunt admission, Amy bit her lip and looked hurriedly away from the man, who had hurt her so much. 'That seemed too obvious.'

'Sometimes the most obvious answer is the true one, *gioia mia.*'

'So, you're suggesting that I house all the animals here?'

'With possibly the ultimate view of eventually taking over the charity and running it from here.'

'I wouldn't know how to run a charity.'

'Someone else more qualified could deal with that while you took care of the shelter and rescue side of the operation,' Sev told her soothingly. 'But that's an option that can be shelved for now, so don't worry about it.'

Amy was frowning and she shook her head in confusion. 'You're talking as though this would be a permanent move for me…but I was only thinking of somewhere as a temporary base from which I could rehome the animals that are left…and then get out of your hair.'

'Amy, you're going to have my baby. Why would I want you to leave again? This place isn't being used right now. The property needs a fresh purpose and if it's giving you and your four-legged friends somewhere to live…'

'You want me to live here *as well*?' Amy gulped at that news and swallowed hard, taken aback by the extent of his plans on her behalf. She turned away, moving in a constrained half-circle as she pondered, her slender body tight with tension.

How could she possibly place her trust in Sev? He had set her up and used her to get revenge on her father, careless of the hurt he inflicted on her in the process. Now, to be fair, he was striving to make amends. She didn't have to forgive him though, did she? But, squirm as she might, right now, Sev was offering her and the dogs their only route to safety and security. Nobody else was likely to make such a proposition and she was painfully aware that not all the current animals would be offered places by other rescue organisations.

'You're giving me a lot to think about,' she muttered ruefully.

'You'll have to be on the spot to care for the animals, and the house is empty but for the housekeeper. I also have a local vet willing to volunteer his services.'

'Oh, do you think there's any chance that he would consider me for a placement?'

'With all you'll have to do here with the animals, I think you need to accept that you won't complete your apprenticeship until *after* the baby's born,' Sev contended. 'It would be too dangerous. You can't take the risk of physically straining yourself or getting injured.'

'But...'

'Nor can you endanger yourself with infections, parasites or working with chemicals or radiation. The vet enumerated the risks. You will have to be very careful working here as it is,' Sev pointed out. 'You'll need help with the animals to keep yourself safe and I will get that organised. You have a hundred tasks to worry about, but in the short term all you should be focusing on is where you live, looking after yourself and the welfare of the animals.'

'But you're doing so much,' Amy whispered in bewilderment. '*Too* much... I can't accept all this.'

'Why not?'

'Because it *is* too much. I'm only in need of a temporary solution while you're talking about more long-term stuff. You don't need to make that size of a commitment because you don't owe me anything.'

'I *do*,' Sev said, catching her restless hands in both of his to stop her moving, and staring down at her with his stunning black-fringed golden eyes. 'This is my way of saying *truly* sorry.'

Disturbed by his proximity and the faintly familiar scent of his cologne assailing her nostrils, Amy jerked her hands free of his immediately. 'Yes, it's a great solution for the animals but I can't agree to come and live here in your house.'

'Even though you would be doing me a favour by agreeing?'

'And how do you make that out?' she demanded as Sev urged her up shallow steps into the cosy interior of a big wood-panelled hall crammed with furniture, books and assorted ornaments and pictures. The effect was more like an overflowing antique shop than an actual home.

'I'll show you round,' Sev told her, throwing open doors as he passed, waiting for her to glance in at a drawing room, a library, a further seemingly endless selection of dining, morning and sitting rooms. 'I've got a housekeeper hiring people to do all the practical stuff like cooking and cleaning and getting bedrooms ready for the guests, but I need someone to declutter the place and make it look more inviting and I've only got two weeks left to achieve that. I think you could give the hall that Christmas gloss that people enjoy at this time of year. That's one reason why I'm asking you to move in now. I believe you could pull this place into better order.'

Amy dragged her fascinated gaze from what looked like a very gloomy Victorian mourning memorial on a marble hearth and swallowed hard. 'Why did you leave all the arrangements to the last minute?'

Sev knew better than to admit that he had

originally planned to entertain his father's family at his London town house. The sudden change of venue was merely a ploy for her benefit to persuade her that he needed something from her as well. 'I've had a lot on my mind recently.' It wasn't a lie. He was discovering that the concept of lying to Amy, even to keep her happy, was a double-edged sword that made him as uneasy as if an innocent fib might lead to him being struck by a divine bolt of retribution.

'We need to talk about this…*properly* talk about this,' Amy told him anxiously as he escorted her up one half of a giant double staircase that would not have looked out of place in a small palace.

'I don't see what's left to talk about,' Sev responded lightly.

'Only money. You're not expecting me to pay you rent, are you?' Amy shot at him ruefully, her cheeks hot.

'Of course, I'm not. Leave money out of this,' he urged impatiently.

'I'm afraid I can't. Who is going to pay

for the feed for the animals and the bedding and the medication if I'm not even working?' Amy pressed, getting down to the nitty-gritty details he would have avoided.

'Me. Charitable venture?' Sev sent her an amused smile. 'Perfect tax write-off.'

Amy grasped that point and recognised why he would seek to have the charity kept alive and based at the house. She was relieved by that reason because it removed some of the guilt that was dogging her. 'But you can't write off the cost of my living expenses.'

'It's my baby. It's my right to look after my baby's mother,' Sev insisted, pushing open a door into a big bedroom.

'The obligation to look after your baby's mother doesn't feature in any law I've ever heard of unless you're married to the lady,' Amy told him gently. 'Look, I understand what you're trying to do here for me, but I don't feel comfortable with your generosity…even though I'm going to *accept* it for the dogs' sake.'

'I'm not expecting anything from you other

than your help with making the house presentable for Christmas. I can have you moved in here within forty-eight hours,' Sev continued. 'I'll organise transport for the animals and your possessions.'

'As far as possessions go, I have a suitcase and that's pretty much it. My boss loaned me the furniture in my room and the mini oven,' she completed prosaically. 'I'm used to travelling light.'

It pained Sev that all she owned would fit in a single case and that she thought nothing of that fact. He compressed his lips and made no comment, watching her investigate the extra doors that led off the bedroom to discover a contemporary bathroom and dressing room, where she poked through built-in wardrobes and drawers, her frown warning him that she was thinking that the contents of one suitcase were unlikely to have much presence there.

Amy walked back out to face him, looking uneasy. 'All right, I'll move in as long as you understand that it's only a temporary thing,' she proffered stiffly.

Sev nodded as if he agreed when he didn't agree, wondering in exasperation why she was the first woman in his life for whom he had had to embroider the truth. The bottom line was getting her moved in and comfortable.

Amy froze as the black SUV that had collected her turned in through giant wrought-iron gates set between tall turrets that punctuated the long stone estate wall she had not noticed on her first visit to Oaktree Hall. Of course, Sev had brought her in through a far less intimidating rear entrance, sparing her the imposing front view of the house at the end of a long dead-straight drive bounded by the big oak trees that had given the building its name. Amy almost pinched herself to see if she was dreaming that she was to move into a house that size. From the starting point of a converted storage room, it was a massive move upmarket for an ordinary young woman.

Only Amy didn't feel quite so ordinary when she was greeted at the front door by the housekeeper, who introduced herself as Martha and announced that she would bring coffee and toasted pancakes to the drawing room to welcome her to her new home.

It's not my new home, she wanted to protest, but it would have been churlish to contradict the smiling older woman, who was, after all, only an employee and probably had not a clue about Amy's true status in Sev's life. When Sev finally wore out his belated attack of conscience, he would surely be glad to see her cut ties and leave, Amy reckoned as she settled down on a faded but well-sprung sofa and awaited her coffee. A log fire was burning merrily in the grate, throwing out brightness and warmth into the big room. Amy stood up again, already mindful of Sev's request that she do something to make the old property look more inviting for his guests. She wandered round the room, mentally labelling what could go and what could stay in terms of furniture and what seemed to be an endless supply of knick-knacks littering every beautifully polished surface.

Martha arrived with a tray and Amy sat down again, listening as the older woman told her that her mother and her grandmother had worked at the hall before her and that she remembered the house when it was still occupied by some elderly aunt of Sev's a decade earlier.

'Maybe you could advise me on what to move out,' Amy remarked.

'I wouldn't know what to choose, Miss Taylor. The old lady liked the place packed because that was what she was used to here. But Mr Cantarelli has sticky labels for you to put on the pieces you want shifted. We've got handymen for the house, who will do the heavy work,' she explained. 'I will pack up the breakables for you and put them in the attic.'

'Sev has everything organised,' Amy responded with a rather tight smile as she lifted her toasted pancake.

'He's the most efficient man,' Martha assured her as she departed again.

Oh, don't I know it? Amy reflected ruefully, sipping her coffee. It was obvious that he didn't want her to flex more than a finger physically, much as though a pregnancy only a handful of weeks along was a seriously heavy burden for a young able-bodied woman. On the upside, though, she supposed it was a good sign for the future and the baby's benefit that he was so keen to ensure that she didn't injure herself or overdo anything.

'Sorry, I had the estate manager with me when you arrived...' Sev announced from the doorway, almost startling Amy into dropping her cup as she swivelled to look at him with wide violet eyes of surprise.

'What are you doing here?' she almost whispered.

'For the moment, I'm staying here too,' Sev admitted, gorgeous dark golden eyes dancing with what might have been amusement at her astonishment.

Amy set down her cup with a clatter on the tray, cursing herself simultaneously for not having immediately noticed that the tray was set for *two* and not one. She jumped up, an angry flush mantling her cheeks. 'Well, that's not going to work, is it?' she snapped. 'We can't live in the same house!'

Sev closed the door and lounged back against it, a tall, commanding figure even in jeans and a sweater, his darkly handsome arresting features clenching hard. 'Why not?' he asked quietly.

CHAPTER TEN

AMY OPENED HER mouth and after a couple of seconds closed it again because, of course, it was *his* house and he was entitled to stay there whenever he liked. 'I didn't realise that you'd be here too when I agreed to move in,' she confessed tightly. 'I assumed you'd be remaining in London.'

'I'm not planning to harass you. It's a very big house,' Sev reminded her gently as he helped himself to the coffee on the tray, as cool as a cucumber in the face of her discomfiture, which only annoyed her more. 'When you're ready, I'll take you out and show you the kennels that have been set up in the barn.'

Amy nodded vigorously, still struggling to adapt to the idea of Sev inhabiting the hall at the same time as she did.

'And then I thought you could choose a tree for the main hall.'

'A tree?' she repeated blankly.

'Christmas tree?' he extended with a slanting, utterly dazzling smile. 'You seem to be in a daze, *cara mia*.'

To avoid further embarrassing conversation, Amy carried her coffee round the room while she scrutinised the furniture. 'I believe you have labels for me to use.'

'You don't need to start work immediately.'

'I like to keep busy,' Amy told him, her heart still pounding from that smile of his, which infuriated her.

Ten minutes later, he was showing her the barn where a long line of sectional metal cages had been set up for the dogs. An outhouse had been turned into a cattery. The only thing left for Amy to decide was where the two rabbits were to go, and she got the impression that Sev would have preferred to decide that for her as well. On her last visit she had given him a list of all the necessities of feed, bedding and basic medication that were required, and those items were already stored in readiness. The animals would be arriving the following day because Harold's son, George, could not wait to make a start on his expansion plans. Her former boss had presented her with a gift card and had urged her to stay in touch while trying to control his curiosity about the exact nature of her relationship with Sev. She had ducked the awkward questions and stayed silent about the baby she was carrying.

Sev tucked her into an SUV and drove her to the other end of the estate where an elderly tenant had a Christmas tree farm. Sev took the axe from the old man and assured him that he could manage to fell the tree on his own. By that stage, Amy was already feeling that she had been exposed more to Sev than was good for her. Getting every scrap of feeling she had acquired for him back out of her head and her heart was her biggest ambition.

'You know, you never talk about your time in foster care,' Sev remarked, disconcerting her with the intimacy of that comment.

'There's not much to say,' Amy said uncomfortably. 'At the time I was hurting so much from my mother turning her back on me. I was in three different foster homes, all short term. Nobody was bad to me, but nobody really cared about me either. Of course, I wasn't willing to let anyone in back then, so I really didn't give anyone a fair chance until Cordy came back into my life and offered me a home. And she wanted me for me, not for the pay cheque that came with fostering me. I was able to talk to her and forgive myself for the mistakes I had made.'

'Do you think you can forgive me enough to talk to me yet?' Sev asked as she trudged behind him over the rough grass separating the trees, choosing to walk to one side below the natural woodland that bounded the field, which meant she was less close to him.

'It would help if you would stop trying to flirt with me or compliment me,' Amy responded tightly.

'Not going to do either,' Sev breathed without remorse. 'I did wrong. I apologised but you won't listen.'

In a sudden rage that came out of nowhere at her, Amy stopped dead and shouted, 'Why would I *want* to listen?'

Sev swung round, his lean, hard features set in tough lines. 'Because I'm trying and you're not trying at all.'

Amy rolled her eyes back at him. 'What is there to try for?' she demanded in frustration. 'Even if you'd told me the truth from the beginning, we weren't going to go anywhere anyway. At heart, you're cold. You don't think of anyone but yourself or someone like your sister, who's part of the charmed circle you live in. You don't live in my world and I'm just a novelty to you. We've got nothing in common.'

'I wasn't expecting Little Miss Sunshine to be this unforgiving...' Sev husked.

And that was that. Amy's arm came up as though she was about to slap him, and he grabbed her off her feet and settled her back against the trunk of an enormous tree. 'Fight with me, then,' he invited provocatively. 'It's better than the sulky silence.'

'I do not *sulk*!' she flung back at him furiously. 'And what's the matter with you? You got what you wanted with my father. You wanted me, you *had* me as well... Game over, Sev!'

'Why is it so damned hard for you to accept that I *still* want you?' Sev raked down at her angrily, rage firing his dark eyes to brilliance. 'Because you don't believe it? Because you're set on protecting yourself? Or is it the truth that you run away when things get tough? Because if that *is* the truth about you, I'll stop chasing you.'

'You said you didn't run after women,' Amy remind him nastily.

That untimely reminder struck Sev like a freight train and he looked down at her, wondering how the hell she lit him up like dynamite ready to explode, because he *never* lost his temper and he had just lost it. He had her imprisoned against a tree trunk and he knew he should let her go, but when he gazed down into those electric violet eyes boldly daring him in that perfect face adorned with that ripe pink pillowy mouth, Sev somehow forgot all about letting her go and kissed her instead.

Amy's eyes were locked to his; she recognised the need, the hunger and the longing there, feeling that knowledge thrum through her trembling body like an intoxicating drum beat. Somewhere in the back of her mind exhilaration flared that he hadn't been lying, that he hadn't been trying to sweeten her up by flirting, that he genuinely *did* want her the way he had insisted he did. For the very first time with Sev since the break-up, Amy felt that she was no longer powerless or a passive victim.

He crushed her mouth under his and her head swam, and her knees quaked and, all of a sudden, he was lifting her up against him and she couldn't get enough of him. It was as though every shred of misery and anger from the past weeks spontaneously combusted in a split second into a passion that couldn't be denied and blazed through her every nerve ending.

Anchoring her to his hips, Sev braced her back against the tree, pushing against the aching throb pulsing at the apex of her thighs until she could feel the long, hard shape of his erection. She moaned at the back of her throat, gripped by that mindless wanting that overcame her when he touched her.

'We should go back to the house,' Sev ground out against her cheek as he freed her swollen lips and struggled to catch his breath again while still rocking against that sensitive part of her and driving her insane with the promise of sensation.

'Stop…and I'll kill you!' Amy startled him as much as she startled herself with that threat, but the overwhelming need that had taken hold of her was that impossible to suppress.

Sev lifted his tousled dark head and looked down at her in wondering appreciation and then, with a ragged, breathless laugh, he tasted her mouth again even more passionately, the expert plunge of his tongue sending paroxysms of wanton excitement travelling through her. He lowered her to the ground, jerked down the zip of her jeans, long wicked fingers delving to her molten core and increasing the madness racing through her veins. Only moments later, wild heart pulsing, she was in the midst of a climax and Sev was hoisting her up against him and bringing her down on him with precision. That sudden thrust lit her up like a firework display inside, excitement leaping and bubbling through her trembling body like a dangerously addictive drug. She didn't know what she was doing, even what she was saying, only that she was sobbing something and she was clutching at his hair and his shoulders as another electrifying orgasm tore through her, making her convulse and shake, every skin cell rejoicing as she heard his groan of completion follow her own.

And then as Sev slowly lowered her back down to planet earth it was time to come back to the real world again, only she could barely face it after what she had done. 'It was just sex… I missed it,' she muttered in feverish excuse.

Yes, and that was *so* convincing an explanation when the only sex she had ever had had been one night with him and he knew it, Amy acknowledged wretchedly. Face burning hot as a bonfire, she righted her clothing, drowning in a pit of shame that she knew she deserved, and then her pride came to her rescue and straightened her shoulders. If she made a mistake, at least she should own it, not run away as he had dared to suggest she might tend to do. The awful truth was that she was insanely in love with Sev Cantarelli even if she couldn't yet spell his name. His coming after her, apologising, showing compassion to the homeless animals had all begun to pierce her defences again. He was fluid and relentless as water in nature, always adjusting to the right level no matter what she did to muster her resistance.

'We should pick a tree before the light goes,'

Sev told her straightforwardly, smoothly picking up the axe again and striding on.

Relieved as she was by his ability to move on after an awkward moment, Amy still wanted to plant a booted toe somewhere it would hurt him. He hadn't said anything, well, she hadn't left him much room to say anything after what *she* had said, she conceded wretchedly, but his silence on that score was somehow worse.

Sev was on a punch-drunk high as he had never experienced before, his body still roaring with endorphins and the recollection of pleasure he had not known existed until meeting Amy. Yes, he had missed her, nothing wrong with that. He was more concerned by an appallingly unfamiliar desire to make Amy's life happy and perfect, a desire that shook him inside out. He wanted her, he wanted the baby. It was a sexual obsession, he labelled it with relief. What else could it be? A full-grown sexual obsession, sufficient to drive him in the direction of the kind of behaviour he had never entertained before.

'That tree is a lovely shape,' Amy mumbled.

Sev didn't even glance at her; he followed the direction of her pointing hand. After all, Amy was blushing enough for both of them. If he didn't watch out, he'd start blushing too. But… *Dio*…it had been *amazing*. Didn't say a lot for his legendary lively womanising sex life that he had never enjoyed that much excitement before, did it? *Madre di Dio*, he wasn't in love, was he? He remembered his half-sibling, Tor, at his wedding with his bride, Pixie, and almost shuddered at the recollection of Tor cheesily telling someone that Pixie *lit up his world*. He didn't feel like *that*, did he? He didn't do love, wasn't ever planning to marry and yet…the thought of Amy doing those things with another man set him on fire with rage. He didn't want to share her with anyone except their child. So, they would live together, he reasoned. His child would be illegitimate; it hadn't done him any harm, had it?

Actually, it *had*, Sev conceded, thinking of all the times as a child that he had wished his mother had married his birth father. When he had got to know his father as an adult, he had done so at a very slow pace. Wary and cynical, he had kept Hallas Sarantos at a distance, refusing to credit that the older man could be as straightforward as he seemed, a happy family man, who had beaten himself up with guilt at the knowledge that he had a son out in the world who was a stranger to him. Over time, Sev's reservations about Hallas had crumbled but, until Amy's advent in his life, he had continued to keep everyone at a safe distance, telling himself that he was doing so to protect his birth father, because Hallas would be devastated if he knew how unhappy Sev had been as a child.

But who knew what lay in his future or Amy's if he didn't marry her? Marriage was a commitment, a binding promise of fidelity and stability. His father had it with his family. Tor had it with Pixie. If he was fair, there *were* examples amongst friends and family who had good relationships, unlike his mother's side of the family tree. Sev tensed momentarily as he was wielding the axe. He was messing up his hands, and he knew it was because he wasn't accustomed to physical work, but there was something oddly satisfying about using his muscles and hacking the hell out of the tree. It was a great deal easier than limping through an emotional wasteland where he had never been before and didn't really want to linger. But if he was thinking about marriage, he had to be realistic and think of stuff he wasn't accustomed to thinking about, label things like feelings that he had never explored before. And he absolutely hated doing it and took his raging frustration out on the tree.

Watching Sev chop the tree down was strangely sexy, Amy acknowledged, her face still hot because after what they had just shared she should not be even thinking along that line again, should she? She shouldn't be thinking of the muscles flexing below that sweater, the taut, flat line of his stomach, the breadth of his chest, the tight neatness of his male hips in denim, the long, long straight legs. Oh, she might as well be honest—*everything* about Sev turned her on and made her react like a silly schoolgirl. She had no control over her eyes or her thoughts when Sev was around, but she had to get a handle on her responses if he was going to be living in the house and she was to have daily contact with him.

That night, the tree trimmed and placed in a giant half-barrel and installed ready for decoration in the cluttered entrance, Amy went up to bed, satisfied that she had kept busy because she had gone through the drawing room with labels and the transformation was on its way. Once the clutter was put away, the house would look much better. Sev had left her in peace to work, a state of affairs she had told herself she was very grateful for, even though she didn't quite believe it after a long bath and climbing into her spacious bed, the comfiest she had ever lain on.

Just as she was reaching out to douse the light, the door opened and framed Sev, clad only in a towel.

In a surge of surprise, she sat up, violet eyes wide and startled. 'Sev...what—?'

'Well, if it's just sex,' he murmured very softly, 'we don't need to stop, do we?'

Unprepared for that approach, and the experience of having her own statement tossed back to her in provocative challenge, Amy stared back at him and knew there was nothing she wanted more than Sev in her bed. A sort of might-as-well-be-hung-for-a-sheep-as-a-lamb outlook gripped her.

The silence hummed and perspiration broke out on her upper lip. 'I suppose not,' she mumbled unevenly.

Not a shy bone in his lean, muscular golden body, Sev dropped the towel and vaulted in beside her. 'So we'll keep it simple,' he told her. 'Just you and me...we're exclusive... OK?'

'OK,' Amy responded sunnily, wondering if he could be so insane as to imagine that, pregnant and ordinary as she was, some other man was likely to want to run off with her, particularly when she had Sev. Who would run out on Sev? Her face fell again. Or did he think she was flighty, a bit easy? Likely to go with the first guy who asked? He was naïve, she decided. Nothing was that simple, particularly with a baby involved.

'We're living here together now,' Sev added.

'Are we?' Amy wondered what it was about Sev that meant he always had to push against her limits, force her that extra mile, throw in something else she hadn't even had time to think about and catch her on the hop. Maybe that was just Sev. Maybe he literally thought in the moment, didn't do all the agonising she did in fear of making a wrong decision.

'Sì...' Sev lapsed into Italian in shock at the commitment he had just made, yet that same statement of intent had not fazed her at all. He marvelled at her calm. She had caught him without even trying to catch him and now he was where he had believed he never wanted to be, he reminded himself grimly, *involved* with a woman in a steady relation-ship for the first time ever, and on some level it scared him to know that, also for the first time ever, he had boundaries to his freedom.

CHAPTER ELEVEN

ONLY TEN DAYS LATER, Amy lowered her maternity jeans while the technician wielded the wand over the little bump that was developing much faster than Amy had appreciated it would. That was the main reason that Sev had got away with kitting her out with an entire new wardrobe, she conceded ruefully, because, with neither income nor clothes that fitted any longer, she hadn't had much choice. Surprised by the rate of her expansion, the consultant Sev had insisted she see had sent her straight upstairs for a scan.

'Oh, my goodness,' the technician carolled in apparent delight. 'Mummy and Daddy are expecting twins…'

Amy went into shock and just lay there like a felled tree, gaping at the screen as two little blips were pointed out. Sev's grip became so taut he was almost crushing her fingers.

'Two…' Sev said gruffly.

A nightmare, by his estimation, Amy thought sadly. One baby was a lot to handle, the prospect of *two* could only strike a resolutely single man as a nightmare. That wasn't how *she* felt but, although she was certain that Sev would not be that frank and hurt her feelings, secretly that had to be how he felt, and she couldn't bring herself to look at him.

'How soon will we know the gender?' Sev asked shakily, the slight tremor in his usually calm voice all too revealing.

It would be quite a few weeks, he was told, and armed with that knowledge they returned to the consultant. In company with the older man, Sev put on a very good show of a man excited to death by the prospect of twins. Amy felt overwhelmed but quietly happy that her pregnancy was progressing well, even though she would also have to worry about a greater risk of complications.

Back in the limo, Sev closed a hand over

hers. 'We'll *have* to get married now. We can't have *two* of them running round without my name,' he told her with unhidden amusement.

'Sev...' Amy murmured quietly, tugging her hand away. 'These days nobody *has* to marry anyone.'

'Sometimes, you're so literal!' Sev groaned impatiently. 'OK, I agree that that wasn't a romantic proposal but let me emphasise the obvious... I'm *not* a romantic guy.'

'We're perfectly happy as we are,' Amy broke in tightly.

'You may be... I'm not,' Sev admitted bluntly, agitated by the lack of permanence to their living arrangements. '*Two kids?* I think we need to get married ASAP.'

Amy breathed in deep and slow. Tears were stinging behind her eyelids. Being pregnant was making her incredibly emotional. The silliest things could make her eyes well up. 'I don't think any woman wants to get married just because she's pregnant,' she told him unevenly. 'I think that if you sit down and really think about that, you'll agree.'

'It's not because you're pregnant…it's all the other stuff as well.' Abruptly, Sev swallowed hard and fell silent, registering that he had presented the idea badly and possibly at the ultimate wrong moment.

'What stuff?' Amy prompted eagerly.

'Us…we work really well together,' Sev told her prosaically, because he literally did not have the vocabulary to describe what he couldn't even interpret for his own benefit. Amy had been living with him for only days, but he already knew that his life was *better* with her in it and that was the baseline from which he worked. How was he supposed to present that to her in a prettier package? He could only suppose that she expected a ring and all that malarkey. As if he was trying to sell himself as a good catch? So, he would buy a ring, take her out for dinner, do it the old-fashioned way, he reasoned, when all *he* wanted to do was marry her yesterday…

Without hesitation, he tugged her gently up against him and splayed a large possessive hand across the slight mound of her stomach.

It was such a turn-on knowing his babies were in there, he reflected with satisfaction. Lean brown hands swept up from her thighs and slid under her top to rise and cup her swelling breasts, his thumbs brushing across the sensitive tips.

And just that easily Amy's body went into sensual overdrive, heart racing, an inner clenching between her thighs, and the shock of that immediate electrifying response made her shudder. She told herself to peel herself off him, but the iron bar of his arousal was obvious beneath her and the wanton part of her, the part of her he had awakened and controlled, just wanted to allow him to go ahead. Even as he bent down and crushed her upturned parted lips under his, sending her heart hammering even faster, she was pulling back in defiance of that weakness, that vulnerability that could make her shiver and shake around him. No power on earth could make her crave anything the way Sev did, but she knew she had to resist and protect herself from putting all her faith in Sev.

She had made that mistake too often in her life, first with her mother, then with Cordy's death when everything had fallen apart for her and then with Harold, who had had no choice in what he had done but whose actions had still ripped away every piece of security she had. How could she now trust Sev? In the end, people always chose to put their own needs and happiness ahead of those of others, and sooner or later Sev would realise that playing house with the woman he had accidentally got pregnant was more of a temporary novelty than a permanent new blueprint for his future. And where would she be then, when he wanted to walk away?

Chilled by that thought, Amy yanked herself away with clumsy determination and took refuge in the opposite corner of the back seat, her face flushed, her breath heaving in her lungs at the effort that severance had demanded from her because, in truth, stepping away from Sev in any fashion *hurt*. She had accepted that, for the moment, loving him was not something she could change. But she did not see a future with him because he didn't feel the same.

He couldn't keep his hands off her, but that was sex and that wasn't enough. He was so generous and good to her in every way that mattered but that wasn't love either, it was merely the way a decent man treated the woman carrying his babies. None of that was sufficient to sustain a marriage, she reasoned wretchedly.

Moving into Oaktree Hall had only plunged her more deeply in love with Sev than ever. She walked into the house by his side, quietly appreciating the changes that she had made. She had eradicated the clutter, the definite Victorian vibe that his elderly aunt had once maintained in the house. The fussier pieces of furniture had been put back into storage as well and what was left would definitely have featured in Oaktree Hall's heyday in the nineteen twenties.

The Christmas tree in the hall looked fantastic. Amy had dug through boxes in the giant attics to find glorious blown-glass antique ornaments and had hung them, supplemented with more contemporary additions. Lights twinkled and glowed over the tree under the light of the fire in the hall and both Harley and Hopper were sprawled on the hearth in front of it. Happiness flooded Amy and she suppressed the regrets licking up underneath because nobody got *everything*.

What she had with Sev right now was perfectly acceptable, she told herself urgently, as long as she also accepted that he wasn't likely to stay with her for ever. Eventually some other, *flashier* woman would attract his interest and she would have to move out and on with her own life, no longer anchored to his. And that was normal because no man stayed for ever with a woman simply because of a contraceptive oversight and sexual attraction, did he?

In exactly the same way not every mother *loved* her child and Lorraine Taylor's lack of interest and rejection had wounded Amy deeply. Even after Amy had settled down again and was living with Cordy, her mother hadn't cared enough to let Amy back into her life. If her own mother hadn't managed to love her, how could Sev ever love her? Or care enough to stay with her in the long term?

Of course, in her opinion, Sev was only pushing out the marriage idea because his family from Greece and his sister, Annabel, were arriving the next day for Christmas. By all accounts, his Greek father, Hallas Sarantos, was a fairly traditional man, who might well *expect* Sev to want to marry the mother of his unborn children. Naturally Sev would want to please his father.

Amy knew all about that kind of engrained seeking of approval with a distant parent. As a young child she had done everything possible to try and win her mother's approval, her *love*, but nothing, not the working hard at school, the obedience or the helping with meals or the cleaning or laundry had provoked one ounce of genuine warmth from her mother, Lorraine. It was little wonder, she now thought as she looked back, that she had gone off the rails in adolescence, because she had lacked that anchor of parental love and caring that would have given her stronger self-esteem. Not that she had done anything *that* bad when she rebelled, she conceded ruefully, but she was still ashamed of skipping school, cheeking teachers for the first time ever and refusing to listen to people who had tried to talk sense into her again.

It had been back then that her dreams of a father who might not know about her existence, who might want her if he found out about her, had begun, only to be shattered by her mother's assurance that he had not even wanted her to be born. It had been an ugly truth, but a truth she had nonetheless seen for herself in her birth father's face that night at the party when he had been confronted with his daughter.

That was something that she and Sev did have in common because, as a child growing up, Sev had also not enjoyed a parent's love. His father might be a warm caring man who loved him now as an adult but Sev would still instinctively seek to gain his approval, Amy reasoned unhappily, because thinking of all the reasons why she *shouldn't* marry Sev when truly she *wanted* to marry him lowered her spirits.

'You've done wonders with this place,' Sev told her as he strode into the drawing room and surveyed its stylish comfort appreciatively.

Amy winced. 'Anyone could have done it. All I did was clear away the clutter,' she pointed out, failing to mention the updated touches she had added, like cushions and throws.

His black straight brows pleated. 'Why do you do that? Always refuse a compliment? Run yourself down?'

Amy shrugged a slight shoulder. 'That's just me.'

'That's just you not thinking enough of yourself,' Sev contradicted, studying her troubled face with concealed concern. 'We'll eat out tonight, so you can put on one of those dresses you never wear.'

'Dresses aren't really practical with animals around,' Amy told him gently, gazing back at him with violet eyes that were wide and soft. 'It's not because I don't like them.'

Sev was so gorgeous that she still wanted to pinch herself to persuade herself that she was not living a dream. But there he stood, the living embodiment of her every fantasy: tall and dark and devastatingly handsome and sexy. She would treasure and cherish every moment she had with him, she told herself, while knowing that real life wasn't like a dream or a fantasy, especially not for an ordinary girl like her.

She had finally learned how Sev spelt his name and had gone online to satisfy her curiosity. That had been a double-edged sword of discovery, she conceded ruefully. Seeing Sev with a wide and varied selection of sophisticated, really beautiful women had done nothing for her ego and had done even less to convince her that he would ever stay with her in the long term.

After lunch, Amy went out to the barn and the animals. To her delight, two of the dogs and one cat had been rehomed since their arrival, but the day before three puppies had been abandoned in a carboard box by the front gate. Word of the rescue shelter at Oaktree had spread and Amy had anxiously warned Sev that more animals would appear if it wasn't made clear that the shelter as such was no longer open to expansion.

'But it *is*. I thought that's what you wanted?' Sev had countered. 'I told the vet we were open for business.'

'Have you considered the running costs?' Amy had pressed, but Sev had only laughed while contriving to get a lead attached to Kipper's collar, who, with attention, was beginning to bite less often. Amy, however, reckoned that it was only Sev who didn't get nipped because Kipper adored him…just as she did, Amy reflected ruefully. Her phone buzzed in her pocket and she lifted it out.

'You have a visitor. I put him in the drawing room,' Martha told her cheerfully. 'He didn't want to give his name, said he wanted to surprise you.'

Amy trudged back towards the house, wondering who it was because she didn't get visitors the way other people did and certainly not playful folk of the kind who might want to surprise her. Gemma had come to see her one weekend with her son in tow and had stayed for lunch, gobsmacked by Amy's new lifestyle and silenced utterly by one appearance from Sev, but there had been nobody else because her long working hours had made it a challenge for Amy to make friends and keep them. Sev had invited close friends of his own to dinner one evening though, and that had gone surprisingly well. At least, Amy had thought it surprising that the guests were all so friendly towards her, but Sev hadn't found it unexpected at all.

Briefly checking her appearance in a hall mirror to see that she was at least clean and presentable, she walked into the large drawing room with her ready smile pinned to her lips. The smile fell from her face entirely when she found herself confronted by Oliver Lawson's frowning visage.

Amy was thrown off balance, her brows pleating, her triangular face losing colour. 'Why are you here to see me?' she asked, shocked into stillness.

'I want you to sign an NDA and I'm prepared to pay you handsomely for doing so,' he revealed with a stiff unconvincing smile, his cold dark blue eyes locked to her with unnerving force.

'I don't know what you're talking about,' Amy murmured uneasily, although she knew that an NDA was a non-disclosure agreement that prevented someone from talking about what the other party did not want to be talked about in public.

'I want your legal agreement that you will never disclose my identity as your father to anyone,' Oliver extended in grim explanation.

Martha appeared and stood in the doorway offering coffee. In a numb voice, Amy dismissed her again. 'I have no wish to tell anyone that you are my father,' Amy told the older man truthfully as soon as the door closed on Martha's exit.

'Excellent,' he responded with unabashed approval.

'But I'm *not* willing to sign anything that guarantees my silence as I don't think you have any right to ask me for that. It's my business if I want to tell people or not,' Amy completed with quiet assurance.

Oliver Lawson shot her a look of immediate anger, his thin features flushing and tightening, giving her the impression that he was a man with a very short fuse. 'I paid your mother to keep her quiet for twenty years!' he slung at her with withering distaste. 'I met my obligations to both of you!'

'I can't comment on the money you gave her, only to say that legally you were bound to contribute to the cost of maintaining your child,' Amy countered stiffly, while she wondered if it had even once occurred to Sev that her father might seek her out to confront her with his angry dissatisfaction at her very existence in the world. 'If my mother chose to keep you a secret that was her choice, but it may not be mine, although to be frank again I have no current desire to mention you to anyone.'

'I want a legal, binding agreement to keep you quiet!' Oliver thundered back at her, moving closer to take up an intimidating stance. 'Do you realise what that vulgar staged appearance of yours has done to my life? My wife is distraught! My marriage is in ruins! As for my *career...*'

Amy squared her shoulders. 'The decisions you made at my birth are not my problem or my concern,' she retorted with dignity. 'I can only speak for myself and I don't think I need to sign anything for your benefit.'

Deep down inside herself, Amy was cringing from the man, whom she so strongly resembled in colouring, while he strode up and down in front of her, angry and desperate. *Her father.* That truth felt surreal because he was so clearly a man to whom the designation of fatherhood meant nothing at all. He wasn't interested in her in any way and was completely divorced from her as another human being related to him by blood. She had already surmised those facts by his reaction to her at the party but his second appearance in her life was needlessly upsetting, she conceded heavily. At the same time, she felt strong enough to stand her ground and honestly state her opinion to the older man, refusing to allow him to visibly upset her because she had her pride, and she had lived over twenty years without her father and knew she could continue doing so without harm.

'Why not? You *need* my money! And if you don't need it now, you soon will.' Oliver Lawson spat out a contemptuous laugh and looked her up and down with scorn. 'Do you really think you're so secure with Cantarelli? You won't hold him more than a few weeks. He'll get bored with you and then where will you be? Out on the street where you belong like every other little gold-digging slut!'

In the same instant as Amy backed away in dismay from that offensive verbal attack, someone pressed her carefully to one side and flashed in front of her. It was Sev, she registered incredulously as he planted a fist in her father's face and sent him flying down onto the rug in a startled heap. 'Don't you *dare* call Amy a slut!' Sev seethed, hauling a groaning Oliver Lawson up by his jacket and evidently ready to hit him again.

Amy yanked at Sev's arm as he raised it threateningly a second time, shaken by his intervention but grateful for it as well. 'No, *don't* hit him again. Just get him out of the house,' she urged shakily.

'You broke my nose!' Oliver Lawson gasped in disbelief, blood staining his shirt front.

'I would like to break every bone in your body but, fortunately for you, your daughter stopped me,' Sev breathed icily, thrusting the older man in the direction of the door while Amy struggled to catch her breath.

Only minutes later she heard a car starting up and she released her breath in a long sigh of relief.

'You hit him…' Amy croaked as Sev appeared in the doorway.

'Not half as hard as I wanted to,' Sev breathed in a raw undertone. 'The bastard! Thinking he could walk into our house and abuse you! And calling *you* a gold-digger? A man who married a woman he didn't love to milk her like a cash cow? I gather he assumed I'd be in London at my office…idiot! I was afraid of something like this happening because he's blaming *you* for his downfall when it's his own lies and extra-marital affairs which have caused his problems.'

A little thrown by that spirited speech and the surprising admission that Sev had feared such an approach on her behalf, Amy sat down because she was feeling somewhat dizzy in the wake of all the excitement. 'You shouldn't have hit him,' she said numbly again. 'Violence is never an answer.'

'But it can be, in certain circumstances, *very* satisfying,' Sev slotted in without remorse. 'When I caught that last sentence and saw him moving towards you, blatantly trying to bully you…and not only are you *my* woman, you're pregnant and even more vulnerable…' He fell silent, compressing his lips as he expelled his breath in a pent-up surge and raked long brown fingers angrily through his already tousled black hair. 'To be honest, I wanted to rip him apart for even daring to come near you! What did he want?'

Amy explained about the NDA and her refusal, concluding by saying, 'Not that I want to mention that we're related to anybody!'

'I'm sorry that you were embarrassed like that and that I put you in the firing line with him without thinking about the consequences at the time,' Sev murmured gravely as he studied her, his lean dark features taut with concern. 'He would never have sought you out if I hadn't brought you to his attention and embarrassed him.'

'But you didn't think that through when you embarked on your revenge project,' she completed for him.

'I wasn't capable of putting myself in your position then. I had zero empathy and tunnel vision,' he acknowledged curtly. 'I just saw that Annabel was hurt and I wanted to hurt him back…but he's not sensitive enough to be hurt in the same way as you are.'

Sev bent down and lifted her where she sat and settled her down again full length along the sofa. 'You still look ill. He frightened you, shocked you. Maybe I should call a doctor.'

'Oh, don't be silly,' Amy parried. 'I was just thinking of poor Annabel having to deal with him all alone that night that she stumbled and fell. He's scary in a temper and I'm ashamed that he's my father. I didn't appreciate until now that what my mother screamed at me about my father the day we rowed *was* genuinely the truth about him. I often thought that she could have said that stuff to punish me and make me more grateful that I had her.'

Sev hovered, still all shaken up but unable to grasp why that was the case in the aftermath of the encounter. He had enjoyed hitting Lawson and throwing him out, but he was appalled by Amy's pallor and distress and the dreadful awareness that he had not kept her safe in their home from such an ugly approach. Indeed, a whole slew of unfamiliar emotions were assailing Sev in a tidal wave in that moment and guilt rose uppermost. He was incredibly protective of Amy and hated seeing her suffer, but it felt much worse to be forced to accept that *his* actions were the direct cause of that suffering. In a blind need to seek revenge for the harm caused to his sister, he had fuelled Oliver Lawson's resentment against Amy and her very survival.

'I triggered his visit with what I did to you at the party,' he murmured flatly. 'I didn't consider the outcome, not for you as his daughter.'

'No, you didn't,' Amy agreed softly. 'And

it did kill any little fantasy I had about my mother having lied about the kind of man he was, but that was for the best.'

His high cheekbones were clenched as hard as granite. 'This whole situation has *hurt* you and I would never have knowingly chosen to do that to you.'

Amy sighed. 'You wouldn't do it *now*. I know that.'

'At the time, I only considered Annabel and I realised once I saw your history that he would never want a relationship with her child either,' Sev proffered hesitantly. 'I am ashamed that I was that arrogant, that insensitive to your feelings as his daughter.'

'I forgive you because you've changed...at least with me,' Amy interposed. 'You lashed out in anger against him and, the way you grew up, that's not that unexpected. You weren't taught to consider other people's needs because nobody considered yours as a child.'

Sev had never put that together for himself and he studied her in surprise, rejoicing in her calm strength, understanding and compassion with an intensity that shook him, his fists knotting as he thought about what a creep her father was and how little she deserved his cruel indifference. And such was the fierce power of his own response in that moment as he looked at her that he understood himself for the first time in weeks and, all of a sudden, everything magically fell into place for him. He swung on his heel and strode out of the room, leaving her staring at the space where he had been, in bewilderment at his abrupt withdrawal from the conversation.

Didn't he believe that she no longer blamed him for that party confrontation with her long-lost father? He hadn't understood what he was doing. He had not foreseen the likely consequences because what was obvious to others was not always obvious to him. An emotionally neglected child, Sev only knew how to protect himself from hurt, and he had buried his emotions deep as a coping mechanism to better handle a callous mother and a resentful stepfather, who had never wanted responsibility for another man's child in the first place.

That was why Sev didn't recognise his own emotions, never mind those of the people around him. He knew the basics and had got by fine on the basics until Annabel had been badly treated and deeper feelings and urges had become involved, and from that point on Sev, in all his magnificent arrogance, had been as lost as the child he had once been. Amy realised that, just as she understood that her own reluctance to trust him came from the anxious insecurity that had dogged her since her mother had abandoned her to foster care.

Sev strode back in, his lean, darkly handsome face taut, and Amy's heart sank because she immediately recognised his tension and feared the source of it. 'What's wrong?' she asked jerkily.

'You would be closer to the truth if you asked what's right,' Sev quipped, his dazzling smile curving his wide sensual mouth as he feasted his stunning liquid-bronze eyes on her and dropped down with fluid drama onto one knee in front of her.

Amy sat up with a sudden start. 'What are you doing?' she gasped, refusing to credit what her brain was telling her.

'Would the marriage proposal be any more acceptable if I told you that I loved you and that that's why I want to marry you?' Sev asked gruffly.

Amy was so revved up with hope by that statement that her skin went clammy with shock, as though she were actually in the presence of a threat. 'Er…possibly, *if* it was true and not just something you're saying to persuade me to do what you want,' she muttered in a rush.

Sev reached for her hand and, with great care, threaded a glittering solitaire diamond ring onto the correct finger. 'It's true,' he assured her squarely, treating her to a warm tender appraisal that literally stole the breath from her lungs.

'It seems very sudden,' Amy remarked in a

brittle undertone, because she was so worked up by the possibility that he might care for her that she couldn't catch her breath.

'Well...' Sev gritted his teeth. 'I think the feeling was there from the very beginning but I didn't understand or recognise it. When you walked out on me after the party I didn't sleep through a single night until I saw you again. I *couldn't* let you go.'

'But you didn't *do* anything!' Amy condemned with helpless bite. 'You sent me stupid flowers and I thought you were being a smartass!'

Sev winced and slowly stood up again, reaching down to catch her hand in his strong grip and tug her upright. 'I am a smart ass a lot of the time,' he conceded, his shapely mouth quirking. 'But not having access to you drove me crazy. I was trying to come up with a magic formula to get you back without losing face, and then we met at the bar and you told me you were pregnant... That was the best news I ever heard because that was a link between us that you couldn't deny.

You were so switched off with me that day though. I thought you might never forgive me for what happened at the party.'

'I was really nervous about how you'd react to the news and you literally showed no reaction at all.'

'I was nervous too… There's nothing like the awareness that you've already screwed up to bring down a smart ass.' Sev groaned. 'I was afraid of saying the wrong thing and very conscious of the way Lawson had reacted to Annabel's news. Everything was too rocky between us for me to risk saying *anything* that could have been misinterpreted as unsupportive.'

Amy tensed. 'Let's admit it wasn't an ideal situation.'

'Yet I wanted that baby from the minute you mentioned it…and two at once, even better. We'll do a much better job… I hope… than our own parents did,' Sev murmured ruefully.

'Most probably because you love me and… I've *always* loved you. I mean right from the start. That's why I hated you so much back then, because I felt like such an idiot for having believed in you, for having credited that someone like *you*—'

Sev laid long fingers against her parted lips, momentarily silencing her need to downgrade herself. 'Someone like me fell madly in love with you without even realising it…and then I felt so *gutted* when I lost you and I couldn't admit that to myself. Everything just felt weird in my life the minute *you* were out of it. It was only for ten days but I wasn't myself for a moment of those ten days.'

'You were unhappy,' Amy said gently. 'Just like I was.'

'I couldn't move on, couldn't get you out of my head,' Sev confided with an unashamed shudder. 'It was horrible. I've never experienced that before with a woman.'

'Not even when you were younger?'

'No. It has always been easy come, easy go with me.' When Sev saw the frown drawing her brows together, he continued. 'I was always honest with women. I didn't cheat on anyone and I was never anything less than respectful. Aside of the sex though, I didn't really distinguish between my partners and I got bored quickly. I thought that that was just me. I assumed that I wasn't a very emotional person and that I would never feel anything more…and then you came along.'

'Yes, I came along and somehow contrived to blow you away,' Amy registered in awe of her achievement.

'You're a much kinder person than I am. That's one reason. We both love animals and hate cruelty. That's another. We both, I assume, like children, even though I somehow thought I'd never have one of my own.'

'And now you're getting two for the price of one and thought that was a good enough reason to get married,' Amy said.

'I want to marry you because I love you and I don't want to imagine my life without you in it. You're giving me a whole host of things I never had before, like your warmth and your sunny outlook and…'

Amy stood up on tiptoe and pulled his head down to her and planted her lips feverishly on his. He took the hint, my goodness, did he take the hint, Amy acknowledged as he pulled her down onto the sofa to kiss her with such hunger that her very toes curled.

'One last confession,' Sev bit out raggedly. 'I twisted the truth when I told you that my family were coming here for Christmas. The original plan was for me to entertain them at the town house, but I needed a reason to keep you here.'

'Twisted the truth?' Amy queried, still breathless from that kiss, her brain working in slow mode. 'You mean, you *lied*?'

'A harmless fib,' Sev bargained. 'I had to persuade you to stay here but I—'

'Also wanted me to believe that you needed me for a purpose, so that I wouldn't feel as though I was freeloading to such an extent,' Amy filled in, wide violet eyes locked tenderly to his. 'Of course, you were planning to use the town house to entertain, not a house that had been unoccupied for years!

Where were my wits? Why didn't I see that for myself? Because I *wanted* the excuse to be useful, because I *wanted* to be in a position where I could do something for you!'

'Even so, I shouldn't have fed you a story.'

'It was that smart-ass gene coming out again,' Amy told him, tugging on his tie to bring his sensual mouth within reach again to claim a slow, deep kiss as her hand ran down over his shirt front, seeking the heat of him, making him shudder. 'I forgive you because I love you.'

'Could we take this upstairs?' he husked.

Wordless in the face of the smouldering hunger burnishing his stunning eyes, Amy simply nodded, her body gripped by the bone-deep craving that only Sev could induce, that tight inner clenching at her core that made her ache. Later she would not recall the passage up to their bedroom, only the breathless excitement of falling back on the bed with a man whose love for her inflamed her on every level. Actually being loved was only marginally more familiar to Amy than it was to Sev, and for both of them that intense sense of connection and mutual understanding, not to mention the sizzling sexual chemistry binding them, was new and gloriously exhilarating.

A long time later, Amy lay back boneless in the bed, her head resting on Sev's chest, her violet eyes languorous as he gazed down at her with appreciation. 'You're going to have to learn to love Christmas,' she warned him.

'I'm pretty sure I already do because I'm *always* going to associate this time of year with finding you,' Sev murmured, with his dazzling charismatic smile lightening his darkly handsome features. 'That places the entire festive season in a much more positive light and, of course, soon we'll have our children to celebrate with, and I think we'll both be making a real effort to make it especially good for them.'

Amy laughed. 'What happened to Mr Scrooge?'

'He fell in love with a waitress, had a renaissance, discovered the secret of happiness.

Dio… I love you *so* much,' Sev confided, flipping her over and under him to study her with adoring eyes.

'Not one bit more than I love you,' Amy whispered, wrapped in a cocoon of contentment and happiness.

EPILOGUE

AMY PUT THE finishing touches of jewellery to her appearance: diamonds in her ears and that once-disputed river-of-diamonds necklace at her throat. She clasped a slender gold watch to her wrist, and she smiled in the fading winter light that had forced her to switch on the lamps. Her sapphire-blue dress was cunningly cut to conceal most of her bump.

Marco and Vito were three now, a pair of very lively little boys who kept her on her toes but, once they had started nursery school, Amy had been keen to extend their family and she was quietly looking forward to the arrival of the little girl she was carrying and wondering with amusement if her daughter would turn into a little tomboy to hold her own with her two older brothers.

Becoming a mother had lifted Amy's confidence almost as much as Sev's love and support had contrived to do. In the spring after that first Christmas together, they had got married in Greece, surrounded by Sev's Greek family, the Sarantos clan. Bowled over by the warmth of their welcome, Amy had soon accepted Sev's family as her own and their wedding had been a wonderfully happy, informal occasion. The twins' birth had been without complication and Sev's father, Hallas, and stepmother, Pandora, had travelled to London to welcome their arrival. Add in the growing closeness between Sev and his half-brother, Tor, who was also based in London and married with young children, and Amy felt surrounded by loving family support, something she had dreamt of all her life but never seriously expected to have. She got on particularly well with Tor's wife, Pixie, who had been a nurse before her marriage.

Sev still had no contact with his mother and stepfather. Amy had seen his mother stare coldly at them both at a charity event, her disdain palpable, and had marvelled at her lack of affection for a son who, to all intents and purposes, she should have been proud to possess. She had been so grateful then that his father's family were so attached to Sev that he had shaken off that encounter with his unfeeling mother without concern, her attitude to him too familiar to be wounding. Perhaps it had made Amy more appreciative of her husband's resilience, but it had certainly made her admire her sister-in-law, Annabel, all the more for having been raised by such a woman and having still turned into a completely different individual.

Annabel, in fact, had steadily grown into being Amy's best friend. The two women had shared a great deal during their first pregnancies, although it had been weeks before Amy finally let Sev's sister into the secret that she was Oliver Lawson's daughter. Annabel had been shocked and then sympathetic, warmly cherishing that extra bond between them, which meant that Amy's twins were even more closely related than cousins to Annabel's little daughter, Sophia. Annabel was currently dating an archaeologist and, although her parents were speaking to her again, relations between them remained cool.

Amy had seen nothing more of her father, and Annabel had had no further contact other than through her solicitor with the father of her child. Oliver's wife had divorced him, and he was no longer CEO of her family insurance company. Her curiosity satisfied on the score of her parentage, Amy rarely thought about the older man. Sev's love and the support of his Greek family were more than enough to keep her feeling secure and appreciated.

Now as she walked downstairs in Oaktree Hall, she spread an approving glance over the festive decorations and the many changes in the house that she had instigated since her marriage. The rooms had been redecorated and the furniture updated until a warm and pleasant ambience between old and new had been created.

Kipper sprang up from the hearth to come and greet her, Harley in his wake. Hopper, old as the hills now, rose more slowly on his three legs and, seeing that Amy was doing the moving, sensibly lay down again rather than tax himself, his little stub of a tail wagging slowly back and forth.

Oaktree Rescue had been launched as a charity a couple of years earlier and under Sev's guiding hand had thrived and expanded to include horses. The stable yard was no longer empty and Sev had taken up riding again. Amy called the shelter his hobby and concentrated her work in the day-to-day running of the operation as well as organising fundraising and rehoming events. They both thrived on being busy but also ensured that they took regular holidays.

Sev came through the rear door in the hall that led out to the back entrance. His black hair was windblown, his jawline stubbled, his riding gear muddy and yet he still took her breath away because he was not one atom less stunning in looks than he had been on the day she married him.

'You're looking...pretty amazing,' Sev

breathed, his dark deep drawl dropping in tenor to one of husky sensuality as he surveyed her standing there below the towering tree, which was awash with ornaments and lights. Slight of build as she was, her pregnancy only showed when she turned to one side and her violet eyes were every bit as riveting as they had been the very first time he saw her. 'I'm glad our visitors won't be here for another hour or so—'

'Annabel's arriving early,' Amy told him gently, warning off the hungry glitter in his gaze even as her own body warmed to that appraisal.

'My sister is marvellous at making herself at home here…as for my father's crew, according to the text I got their flight's running late.'

Two identical little boys in riding gear bowled through the front door, both of them blond and dark-eyed with their father's bone structure. They were squabbling about who had got through the wide door first, their competitive edge well honed since babyhood.

In their wake came their nanny, Ellie, who had been living with the family since the twins' birth, freeing up Amy and allowing her to work.

As Sev was engulfed by his enthusiastic sons he told them firmly, 'Bath…supper…bed…story…' in a familiar mantra to which neither was listening, and Amy laughed as Marco and Vito burbled in frantic excitement about Santa Claus visiting some kids on Christmas Eve to leave the presents early.

'He's definitely not coming *here* early,' Sev assured them straight-faced.

'No?' Marco begged in disappointment.

'No,' Amy declared with finality. 'If we get any presents, we will be opening them tomorrow on Christmas Day.'

'If?' Vito queried in horror.

Ellie bundled the twins upstairs, still complaining. Sev drew Amy into his arms. 'It's going to be another wonderful Christmas, *cara mia.*'

Amy breathed in the fresh outdoorsy scent of him and felt her heart race as their eyes collided. 'Did your hotline to Santa tell you that?'

Sev grinned. 'No. Just looking at you told me that.'

He kissed her and she fell into that kiss like melting ice cream on a sunny day, her whole body thrilling to that sudden surge of passion.

'I need a shower,' he breathed raggedly, his body hard and urgent against hers.

'I'm already dressed,' she moaned with a quiver.

'I'm insanely in love with you,' Sev muttered against her cheek.

Amy flexed against his lean, muscular length and whispered, 'I love you too. Twenty minutes,' she negotiated.

'Not long enough,' he told her, demanding another devastating kiss before urging her upstairs. 'It takes time to appreciate you. I'm not a twenty-minute guy.'

Amy laughed, and fenced back with examples of past stolen moments. They disappeared into their bedroom with Sev still flexing his healthy ego, but by then he was laughing as well, grinning down at her, still utterly enchanted by her sparkling sunny nature. 'Little Miss Sunshine' he had cynically labelled her early in their relationship, never dreaming that she was exactly what he needed most in his life.

* * * * *

LET'S TALK

Romance

For exclusive extracts, competitions and special offers, find us online:

- facebook.com/millsandboon
- @millsandboonuk
- @millsandboon

Or get in touch on 0844 844 1351*

For all the latest titles coming soon, visit millsandboon.co.uk/nextmonth

Want even more
ROMANCE?

Join our bookclub today!

'Mills & Boon books, the perfect way to escape for an hour or so.'

Miss W. Dyer

'Excellent service, promptly delivered and very good subscription choices.'

Miss A. Pearson

'You get fantastic special offers and the chance to get books before they hit the shops'

Mrs V. Hall

**Visit millsandbook.co.uk/Bookclub
and save on brand new books.**

MILLS & BOON